"I have a proposition for you."

Lexie leaned toward Nick, her voice low. "When was the last time you had a *really* good time?"

Words stuck in Nick's throat. His pulse pounded in his temples and in his groin. He was close to giving in. Too close.

"It doesn't matter," he said. "I have a business to run and I can't be distracted."

She smiled with a sly, knowing expression and rose. "All right, Nick. You've made up your mind and I respect that. For now." She moved to the door and looked over her shoulder at him, that same self-assured smile still in place. "And just so you know, I'll be making every effort to convince you to change your mind."

He swallowed hard. "You don't need to do that."

"Oh, but I do." The smile broadened. "Six months is a long time. I hate to think of spending all that time alone, don't you?"

Blaze™

Dear Reader,

Like many of you, I'm a voracious reader. Of course, I adore romance books, but I also read nonfiction, history, mystery and suspense. I'm a big fan of private eye stories. Any time the old movie *The Big Sleep,* with Humphrey Bogart as P.I. Philip Marlowe, shows up on TV, I'm there!

So I had tremendous fun writing my own private eye, Nick Delaney, in this book. Of course, he required a heroine who was up to any challenge he might throw at her, so I created Lexie Foster, a woman intent on taking every advantage of the second chance she's been given in life.

This is also the first time I've mixed a little mystery with my romance in a book. I hope you'll enjoy the results.

I love to hear from readers. You can write me at P.O. Box 991, Bailey, CO, 80241, or e-mail me at Cindi@CindiMyers.com. And be sure to visit my Web site at www.CindiMyers.com for all the latest news.

Until next time…

Cindi Myers

Books by Cindi Myers

NO REGRETS
Cindi Myers

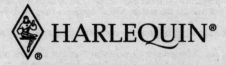

HARLEQUIN®

TORONTO • NEW YORK • LONDON
AMSTERDAM • PARIS • SYDNEY • HAMBURG
STOCKHOLM • ATHENS • TOKYO • MILAN • MADRID
PRAGUE • WARSAW • BUDAPEST • AUCKLAND

For Diane and Mike

ISBN 0-373-79245-X

NO REGRETS

Copyright © 2006 by Cynthia Myers.

1

SOME PEOPLE THINK LIFE is full of second chances. But the way Lexie Foster saw it, do-overs didn't come around that often. When you got the chance for one, you'd better grab it and make it good.

Or so Lexie tried to explain to her best friend, Candace French, as they lingered over frozen macchiatos on a mid-June afternoon in the coffee shop of the building where they worked in downtown Denver.

Where Lexie *used* to work, that is.

"Call me dense, but I'm just not getting this," Candace said as she stabbed a straw into her drink. "Your first day back at work since the accident and you quit? Why?"

"I never liked working at Culpepper and Piper." Lexie took a long pull on the macchiato, savoring the rich caramel and coffee flavor. She'd never really appreciated things like good coffee drinks before, but those days were over. "I've wasted too much time already in that dead-end job," she explained. "The accident taught me that life is too precious to waste a second of it."

She didn't remember much about the accident itself, but the feelings surrounding the night lingered: the heart-stopping terror as she felt her car begin to slide on the icy road and watched it hurtle toward the guardrail; the confusion as she tried to see the ambulance lights pulsing somewhere to her left through a haze of blood, garbled voices shouting unintelligible words; the bleakness that washed over her upon waking in the stark white world of the hospital, unable to move; the incredible joy when they'd released her restraints and she'd discovered she would fully recover; the desire to get out into the world and experience everything that had consumed her during almost six months of rehab.

She sucked up more of the macchiato with a satisfying slurp and looked at Candace. "I'm going to do all the things I was too timid or busy or lazy to do before."

Candace looked skeptical. "What kind of things?"

"I've made a list." Lexie opened her purse and pulled out the little red leather notebook she'd bought especially for this purpose. "I've written one hundred things I intend to accomplish."

Candace opened the book and scanned the first page. "Have affairs with at least six men before I'm thirty?" Her eyes widened. "That's only three years."

Lexie flushed. "That's one every six months."

"You haven't had that many relationships in six years. Have you?"

She shook her head. "That's the whole point. I'm not going to live the way I did before." The "old" Lexie had been conventional, conservative and too concerned about what other people thought of her to take many chances. The "new" Lexie reasoned that life was too short to let anyone else's rules dictate how she should live.

"But six? Don't you think that's a little ambitious? Maybe you should start slowly and work up."

She smiled. "You haven't read the rest of the list."

Candace flipped through the book, her eyes widening as she read. "What? You can't be serious."

"Why not?"

"I've always thought of you as, well, conservative. Reserved."

"I was. I'm not going to be that way anymore."

Candace cleared her throat and glanced at the book again. "Have sex in a public place? Do something kinky?" She fanned herself. "That must have been some near-death experience."

Lexie shifted in her chair. "Those are fantasies. Don't you have fantasies?"

"Yes, but I don't write them down and set out to make them come true."

"Then maybe you should."

Candace returned the book to Lexie. "Maybe you're right. And it sounds like you're going to have a lot of fun. But what does this have to do with quitting your job?"

She tapped the cover of the book. "Number four on the list—no more settling for boring and conventional just because it's convenient. I'm going to find a better job. One that's more exciting, or at least interesting."

"Such as?"

"I saw this ad in the Sunday paper. It's perfect." She took out the clipping from the *Denver Post* and showed it to Candace.

"Private detective seeks administrative assistant. Must be organized, computer literate and have superior phone skills." Candace frowned and returned the clipping to Lexie. "It's still a secretary. It'll probably turn out to be just as boring as what you're doing now. And not as well-paid."

Lexie shrugged. "If I don't like it, I'll find something else. Number eighteen on the list."

"Which is?"

"Embrace change as good."

"Uh-huh. Then what about ditching the scarves?"

Lexie touched the paisley silk scarf knotted at her neck. "I will. I'm just waiting for the scars to fade a little more."

Candace shook her head. "They're not that bad."

Lexie made a face. "They look pretty awful to me." The doctors had to insert a breathing tube in her throat to save her. That and the surgery to repair the resulting hole had left scars that stood out white against her olive skin. Every time she looked in the mirror she cringed.

"So what about all these men you're going to have affairs with?" Candace asked. "Are you going to keep your neck covered while you're making love? Or turn out all the lights?"

"It won't matter so much with them. I'll have my mind on other things." At least she hoped that would be the case.

"Where are you going to find these men?" Candace asked.

"They're everywhere." Lexie smiled. "I'm sure I won't have any trouble finding them."

"No, you won't." She leaned over and patted Lexie's hand. "I'm really proud of you. You go. Wow 'em all."

Lexie tried to look more confident than she felt. It was one thing to sit at home at night and conjure up all these fantasies, quite another to go out and make them into reality. But she'd promised herself she'd do this. Almost dying had made her see how much she'd cheated herself by always playing it safe. Time to take a few chances and *really* live.

NICK DELANEY GROANED and leaned back in his chair after interviewing yet another ditzy young woman who chewed gum the entire time and appeared incapable of alphabetizing correctly. That's what he got for expecting to find a competent assistant on the salary he could afford.

He shifted his gaze to the stack of mail on the corner of his desk. Bills, mostly. Some junk mail. Maybe even a new client or two, but between working cases and trying to find someone to help him in the office, he hadn't time to read his mail. Every day he didn't have an assistant was a day he was likely losing money.

A knock on the door reminded him he had more interviews to conduct. He only hoped one of these applicants was at least mildly qualified. "Come in," he called, sitting up straight.

A looker in a black skirt and sleeveless purple blouse walked in. She had short dark hair, and wore expensive-looking gold earrings and a black silk scarf knotted at her throat. The impression she gave was a combination of sophistication and sexiness—a definite cut above the candidates he'd seen so far.

He rose to greet her, his gaze dropping to her legs, which were long and sleek. Very nice. But could she handle a computer?

He offered his hand. "I'm Nick Delaney. And you are?"

"Lexie Foster." She sat in the chair across the desk and crossed her legs at the ankles. She wore ankle-strap high heels, a particular favorite of his.

He cleared his throat and focused his attention on the résumé she'd slid across the desk. He hadn't been in Denver long enough to start dating anyone, but clearly he was overdue for some female companionship. His ex-wife had rid him of the idea of wasting his time on anything long-term, but there was a lot to be said for momentary gratification. A good lay might help him keep his mind out of the gutter and on his work.

His eyebrows rose as he read Lexie's résumé. If everything on here was true, she was more than qualified for the position. "This says you're currently employed at Culpepper and Piper."

She nodded. "Yes. I've been with them for five years."

He didn't know a lot about the company, but you couldn't miss their imposing glass-and-steel headquarters downtown. They were a high-tech success story, and reportedly one of the top-rated employers in Denver. "Why are you thinking of leaving them?"

She smiled, brown eyes dancing with amusement, as if she were in on some private joke. "I'm looking for more interesting work."

Ah. He'd heard that one before. He folded his hands and gave her a hard look. "People think P.I. work is interesting. It's not. It's deadly dull. I need someone to answer the phone, file paperwork and maybe do background research for civil suits, divorce cases, insurance scams, things like that. Nothing exciting."

He was purposely trying to intimidate her, but she wasn't buying. She crossed her legs at the knee, giving him a look at a good six inches of firm thigh. He kept his expression neutral, but below the belt there was a definite response.

"Working for a large firm like Culpepper and Piper is very impersonal," she said. "I'd enjoy the chance to work one-on-one in a small office."

He shifted in his chair, thinking about the kind of "one-on-one" activities he obviously hadn't enjoyed enough of lately. "You know I can't afford to pay you what you're making now."

"That's all right. I'm sure we can come to some agreement."

Was she intentionally coming on to him, or was his horny imagination taking over? He studied her for clues, but she sat there, serene and perfectly relaxed, her posture almost prim, except for the short skirt and sexy shoes and the ends of the scarf trailing over her breast like a flag marking a hazard.

Working with her might be a hazard to his concentration. Then again, he was desperate for someone competent to help him in the office. He glanced at the stack of mail on the corner of his desk. Did he hire the only qualified person he'd interviewed so far who was willing to work for the salary he could afford, or did he waste more time trying to find someone else for the position?

He looked at Lexie again. "When can you start?"

Her smile widened, positively dazzling now. "I can be in first thing tomorrow."

He nodded, a little breathless in the face of thatsmile. He struggled to his feet and shook her hand, then watched her leave the room, his eyes focused on her curvy bottom in that tight skirt. He knew plenty of guys who'd count themselves lucky to have just hired a secretary this sexy.

But those were guys who hadn't spent the last year digging out from under a fiasco of a failed marriage. Guys who hadn't learned how dangerous a really sexy woman could be.

LEXIE SET THE BUD VASE on the corner of her desk and stepped back to admire the single pink rose she'd bought on the way to work this morning. From now on, she wanted flowers on her desk every day. Today, her first at her new job, was special and called for a rose, but other days she might have carnations or daisies. The kind of flower didn't matter so much as treating herself to that little bit of extra beauty.

She looked around the front office space of Delaney Investigations and couldn't suppress a thrill of excitement. It was happening. She really was changing her life. No more sitting back and dreaming about what could be. Now she was all about making things happen.

She smoothed a hand over her new gray tweed dress. The dress and the matching cropped jacket were made of a conservative fabric, but were cut to cling to every curve. No more dull clothes for her. Now she was a real bombshell with a whole closet full of pencil skirts, fitted jackets, bustiers and designer diva fashions.

The door to the back office opened and she turned to greet Nick Delaney. Though landing a hunk for a boss hadn't been on her list, she had no complaints. Nick looked exactly like the image of a private investigator she'd always had in her mind: dark hair and eyes, broad shoulders, ruggedly handsome features. He hadn't smiled much so far; at times he was almost surly, but there was no real anger in his grumpiness. If this were a movie, he'd be a better-looking Humphrey Bogart and she'd be the femme fatale who stole his heart. It was fun to pretend to play the part. "Can I get you something, Nick?"

"I need a letter typed." He handed her a sheet of paper

on which he'd scribbled an address and a few figures. "It's a bid to do background checks on potential employees. It needs to go out this afternoon. There's stationery and envelopes in the supply cabinet."

"Sure, I'll get right on it." She took the paper and walked over to the computer, aware of his eyes on her. She knew the combination of tight skirt and high heels drew attention to her figure but then, that was the idea, wasn't it? No more blending into the background for her. And she couldn't say she disliked the idea of Nick being attracted to her. After all, he was good-looking and apparently single—there were definitely sparks between them.

She sat and rolled her chair up to the desk. "Is there anything else?" she asked, deliberately keeping her voice low and sultry.

He blinked and she suppressed a smile. "Make a copy for the files while you're at it," he said.

She nodded. There weren't many files so far. She'd checked. In fact, everything about the place indicated Nick hadn't been in business long. "How long have you been a private eye?" she asked.

He frowned and she thought he was about to tell her to mind her own business. But he said, "A little over a year. Before that I was a cop."

"In Denver?" She opened the word processing program on the computer.

"Houston."

She thought she'd detected a bit of a Texas drawl. Very nice.

"As long as we're asking questions, I've got one for you."

Her stomach gave a nervous shimmy. Did he intend to interrogate her? She had nothing to hide. She looked up, meeting his gaze. He had amazing blue eyes, pale against his tan skin. "What would you like to know?"

"Your name. I've never known anyone called Lexie before."

"It's short for Alexandra. But no one calls me that, not even my mother."

He nodded, apparently satisfied, and turned to go into his office. She wanted to ask him to stay, to talk a little longer. She'd like to get to know him better, but she supposed that would come in time. She hated to waste time these days. She had so much she wanted to accomplish, she was impatient to take care of one item on her list and move on to the next.

The letter was done in ten minutes and she took it in for his signature. He was on the phone when she entered, and signed without comment. So much for continuing their conversation.

The rest of the morning passed with agonizing slowness. She straightened magazines and watered the lone rubber tree in the corner of the office. With nothing else to do, she took out the Spanish textbook she'd recently purchased and began leafing through that. Tonight she started Spanish classes at Red Rocks Community College. Number seventeen on her list.

Shortly before noon, Nick emerged from the office and walked straight to her desk. Startled, she slammed the book shut and shoved it into a drawer. "Did you need something?" she asked.

"Do you have plans for lunch?"

"No." She'd thought about walking to the fast-food place on the corner and bringing something back here. Maybe he'd like her to bring him something, too.

"Good. You can come with me. Seeing as it's your first day, I thought I should buy you lunch."

Not exactly an invitation to a hot date, but she'd take it. She took her purse from the desk drawer and stood. "That would be great."

They went in his car—a Ford Explorer that had seen better days. He had to sweep out a litter of food wrappers and convenience-store coffee cups before she could climb into the passenger seat. "Sorry," he mumbled. "One of the things about doing P.I. work is you tend to live out of your car."

She fastened her seat belt, then picked up a key map and a telephone directory off the floor. "I guess you use these in your work."

He nodded and stashed the books behind the front seat. "There's a telephoto lens, binoculars and a cell phone charger down there somewhere, too."

"Tools of the trade," she said.

"That's right."

They headed south from the office on Colfax, past tattoo parlors, pawn shops and funky boutiques, to Vick's, a six-table café wedged between a liquor store and a mini-mart. "It's not fancy, but the food is good," he said as he ushered her inside.

The first thing she noticed was all the cops—two sheriff's deputies, three police officers and a man with a federal badge filled the tables. "Is this some kind of cop hangout?" she whispered as she slid into a chair across from Nick.

"Yeah. We know where all the great dives are."

His grin startled her—all white teeth and a light in his eyes that stole her breath. She'd thought he was handsome before, but smiling, he was transformed. The word devastating came to mind.

The waitress arrived and they ordered from the menu that was written on a chalkboard posted on the back wall—a burger for Nick and a Greek salad for Lexie.

"Why did you decide to quit being a cop and become a P.I.?" she asked when they were alone again.

He picked up his fork and began turning it over in his hand. "It's a long story."

She spread her napkin in her lap and gave him an expectant look, saying nothing. She'd learned that if you kept silent long enough most people would say something to fill it.

He took a long drink of iced tea, then set it down with a loud thump. "You really want to know?"

She nodded.

"I was married. One day I came home and found all my stuff packed in boxes and suitcases in the front hall. My wife asked me to move out." His voice was calm, but the lines around his eyes deepened and his knuckles whitened on the hand that held the glass.

"That's pretty cold," she said, trying for sympathy without pity.

"Yeah, well, she said she'd been trying to let me know how unhappy she was, but I was so wrapped up in work I hadn't noticed, so she figured kicking me out was one way to make sure I got the message."

Give the woman points for being direct. "What did you do?"

"I was stunned. I really hadn't had a clue. I got a room at a cheap hotel and promised her I'd make things better. Since she seemed to think my job was part of the problem, I quit. I decided being my own boss offered more flexibility and better hours."

Wow. He must have *really* wanted to save his marriage. She couldn't imagine loving someone enough to make that kind of sacrifice. "But it didn't work?"

He shook his head. "Nope. Turns out the problem wasn't really my job—it was her boyfriend who'd lost *his* job and wanted to move in with her."

She winced. "Ouch."

The waitress delivered their order. The salad looked delicious. "Why didn't you go back to your old job when things didn't work out with your wife?"

He poured ketchup over his fries. "By then I kind of liked the P.I. business. No office politics, make your own hours. It was a good fit for me."

"Okay, then why Denver?"

He shrugged. "I knew a few people up here. The climate's good. It seemed like a good place to start over."

She nodded. "I guess I can see why you wouldn't want to stay in Houston."

"Your turn. Why did you quit Culpepper and Piper and come to work for a one-man detective agency?"

She speared an olive on her fork and swiped it through a pool of dressing. "Kind of like you, I guess. I'm starting my life over."

He paused, the burger halfway to his lips. "Divorce?"

"Another D word—death."

He set down the burger and stared at her. "Run that one by me again?"

She laughed. "I didn't really die, but almost. I lost control of my car on an icy road and went over an embankment. Apparently I was in a coma for a week. Then I was in rehab for almost six months. When I was finally well I promised myself I was going to live the kind of life I'd always wanted to live. Instead of dreaming about things I'd do 'one day,' I was going to do them now."

"What kind of things?"

"Getting a different job, for one. A new wardrobe. Trying new things. I signed up for a Spanish class at Red Rocks. I want to go to Spain, and lots of other places. I want to learn gourmet cooking."

"That's a lot of stuff."

"There's more. I actually made a list of one hundred things I intend to do."

"You wrote them down?"

She nodded. "I have them all in a red leather notebook in my purse."

"You sound pretty determined."

"Oh, I am." Their eyes met, and she felt the electricity between them again. She couldn't remember the last time she'd been this attracted to a man.

The fact that he was her boss made things a little complicated, but it wasn't as if this was a big company where one or both of them could fall prey to office gossips or even legal entanglements. It was just the two of them, in the office together every day. Anything could happen with that kind of intimacy.

Was that good or bad? The old Lexie would have thought it was bad.

She smiled to herself and finished the last of her salad. Right now, she thought, maybe it was a very good thing indeed.

2

NICK LEANED BACK in his desk chair and admired the view through his open office door. Lexie was doing something with the fax machine, bent over at the waist with her back to him, presenting an enticing view of her rounded backside and long legs. Today she was wearing a black knit dress, belted at the waist, a black-and-white scarf knotted at her throat. She must collect scarves the way some women bought shoes. She'd worn a different one every day this week.

She bent farther over the fax and his eyes traced a line over the curve of her bottom, down her thighs. His fingers curled against his palm as he imagined stroking her there. He was getting a hard-on watching her like this; he felt like a cross between a horny teenager and a twisted voyeur. Every day when he left work he told himself he was going to go out and find a woman and let off some of this sexual steam. Unfortunately, no woman he'd seen lately turned him on the way the one working in his office did, which left him where he'd started—watching and wanting and not doing a damn thing about it.

He told himself he ought to close the door so he could get some work done, but he was enjoying himself too much at the moment.

Hiring Lexie was one of the best decisions he'd made in a long while. She was efficient and intelligent as well as good-looking and sexy. And she was good company, pleasant and easy to be around. He looked forward to coming to the office every morning, knowing he'd see her.

Of course, having her around did interfere with his work to a certain extent. His mind might be determined to focus on the job, but when Lexie was around his body invariably reminded him that he was a healthy man who'd been alone for a while now.

Much as he was tempted to start something with her, he knew it was a bad idea to mix business with pleasure. He'd settled on the unsatisfactory compromise of admiring her when she wasn't looking, and keeping his distance otherwise.

He doubted she'd stay with him long anyway, not with all her talk about wanting more adventure in her life. He'd been like that himself once, when he'd first joined the police force. He'd gotten over that restlessness soon enough. Now he wanted to be settled somewhere, taking comfort in the everyday routine. He hoped Denver was going to be his home for a long time but it was too soon to tell.

The front door opened and a well-dressed man entered. Lexie greeted him with one of her hundred-watt smiles, leaving the man with a slightly dazed expression on his face. He followed her toward Nick's office, clearly mesmerized.

Nick straightened and faked interest in the paperwork spread out on his desk. "Mr. Delaney, Mr. Wittier is here to see you."

Stan Wittier, executive vice president of Carruthers Manufacturing, looked much less imposing in person than he'd sounded on the phone. When Nick stood to greet him, he noticed he was a good six inches taller than the executive, who was a slight man with thinning brown hair and worry lines across his forehead. "Please sit down, Mr. Wittier. Would you like some coffee?"

"Your secretary already offered, but it isn't necessary." He turned to watch Lexie leave, only facing Nick again when the door was closed. He looked disappointed to see her go. Nick didn't blame him.

He sat at his desk again. "On the phone you indicated you wanted to see me because of concerns about your wife?"

Wittier nodded. "Yes. I believe she's being unfaithful."

"What makes you believe this?"

The frown lines deepened. "Ellen is a very beautiful woman, some years younger than myself. Lately I've had a sense that she's restless and bored. In my experience that is a sure sign a woman is considering an affair."

Nick found this an odd choice of words. "Considering, or involved?"

"By now I'm sure she's involved. It's a familiar pattern." Wittier crossed his legs and leaned toward Nick. "I've seen it in my first wife and in the wives of my two business partners. Women reach a certain age and become dissatisfied with their lives. An affair seems to be the answer."

The theory was new to Nick but maybe Wittier was on to something. Maybe the problem in Nick's own marriage hadn't been him or his job at all. Maybe his wife merely had reached "a certain age." "And you want me to verify if your suspicions are true?"

"Yes." Wittier straightened. "I want to find out now and divorce before too much damage is done to my reputation."

"Of course." Nick took out a notebook and pen, prepared to write down the particulars. He loathed these kind of cases, but accepted they were the bread and butter of the P.I. business. "You say your wife's name is Ellen?"

"Yes. I've brought her picture, and a copy of her engagement calendar for the next month, as well as my own schedule." Wittier took these items from his briefcase.

The man's preparedness surprised Nick. "Have you had your wife followed before?"

"My first wife. As I told you, this is a familiar pattern to me."

Wittier's coldness repelled Nick but he didn't have to like people to take their money. Sometimes the dislike even made it easier. "I'll need a deposit. I work on a per diem for this sort of thing, plus any unusual expenses, such as travel. I'll provide an itemized accounting to you. If your suspicions are true, it shouldn't take more than a few days to confirm them."

"I'm familiar with how this works and I'm prepared to write you a check today."

Wittier didn't flinch at the fee Nick quoted, which made him wonder if he should have asked for more. He took the deposit the executive paid and put it in the drawer, then promised to get to work right away.

When Wittier was gone, Lexie came into his office. "You don't look very happy," she said. "Did he not hire you?"

Nick leaned back in the chair and frowned at the drawer where he'd slipped the check. "He hired me. To find evidence that his wife is cheating on him."

She wrinkled her nose. "What has she done to make him think she's cheating?"

"She's 'restless' and apparently behaving exactly the way his first wife did when she was cheating on him." Not much to go on, but then, Wittier knew his wife better than Nick. If Wittier thought she was up to something, she probably was.

"That doesn't sound like much evidence to me," Lexie said.

"Which is why he hired me. He needs concrete proof so he can divorce her and, I suspect, avoid paying through the nose for the privilege."

"How lovely."

He shrugged. "It pays the bills. Yours and mine."

She looked thoughtful. "I guess so. Is it okay if I go to lunch now?"

"Sure. Where are you going?"

"I'm meeting a friend at Jose O'Shea's." She smiled at him, a look that never failed to make him feel a little less weighted down. "Want me to bring you something?"

"That's okay, but thanks." What kind of "friend" was she meeting? A boyfriend? For a second, he had the absurd idea to follow her to see, but immediately dismissed it. What did it matter to him if she was seeing one man or ten?

"Okay. See you in an hour."

He watched her leave, breathing in the lingering scent of her floral perfume. He'd thought he might drive somewhere and buy a burger or a sandwich, but now that Lexie was gone off to meet her mysterious luncheon companion, he found he'd lost his appetite.

CANDACE WAS WAITING at a booth when Lexie rushed in. "Sorry I'm late," she said. "We had a client and I had to wait for him to leave."

"A client. Sounds like business is picking up."

"Nick's new in town." She slid into the booth and helped

herself to a fresh tortilla chip from the basket in the middle of the table. "Things will get better. Besides, when things are slow I can study."

"How are the Spanish lessons coming?"

She shook her head. "Not so well. I don't seem to have much of a knack for languages."

"Hang in there. You'll pick it up eventually."

She nodded. "I will. I'm determined to speak the language by the time I go to Spain."

"And when will that be?"

"This fall, maybe? I think I can have the money saved by then."

"That's amazing to me, considering the pittance this detective is paying you."

"It's not that bad. And I still have some insurance money left from the accident."

The waitress came to take their orders, then the conversation resumed. "Speaking of work," Candace said, "guess who they hired to take your place?"

"Who?"

"A man. His name's Charles Lewis and he's gorgeous and single."

"Then I'm sure he was immediately the most popular person in the office. Is he straight?"

"Apparently so. I should introduce him to you." She crunched a chip. "He might be the perfect candidate for the first affair on your list."

Lexie shook her head. "I've already found the man I want."

Candace leaned toward her, expression eager. "Who?"

"My new boss, Nick Delaney." Lexie tried to keep the triumph out of her voice, but failed. The look on Candace's face was worth all the pain of keeping her plans a secret until now.

"Are you crazy?" Candace said. "He's your boss."

"And he's perfect." Lexie ticked off the reasons on one hand. "He's recently divorced and definitely not interested in any kind of serious relationship right now. He's hard-nosed and practical. And he's gorgeous and sexy."

"Do you think he's interested?"

She smiled, remembering how Nick always watched her when he thought she wasn't looking. "Oh, he's interested."

"Has he said anything?"

She shook her head. "And I don't think he will. Which is why *I'm* going to proposition *him.*" She'd made the decision last night after realizing that in over a week on the job, Nick had been nothing but an absolute gentleman. She was pretty sure he wanted her, but just as sure the practical, sensible side of him she so admired didn't intend to let him do anything about the attraction. If she was really going to have an affair with Nick, she'd have to make the first move.

"What, you're just going to walk up to him and say, 'Let's sleep together. How about it?'"

On these words the waitress arrived with their lunch. She gave Candace a puzzled look, then left them with their enchiladas.

When they were alone again, the two friends burst out laughing. "Seriously," Candace gasped when she'd regained control. "How do you bring up a subject like that?"

Lexie spread sour cream over her food. "I'll simply point out that we're obviously attracted to each other, and that I'm interested in a sexy affair with no strings attached.

I'll explain that I plan to leave for Spain in about six months, so he doesn't have to worry about long-term commitments, and I'll reassure him that I won't let our private relationship interfere with my work at the office."

"It sounds as exciting as negotiating a lease agreement for a car." Candace sliced into her beef enchiladas with the side of her fork. "So when are you going to do this?"

"Friday after work, I think. That will give us the whole weekend to get to know each other." Lexie grinned. "We'll be great together, I just know it."

"Aren't you forgetting one thing?"

"What's that?"

"A lot can happen in six months. What if you fall for this guy?"

Her stomach quivered, but she ignored it. "It won't happen. Neither of us is interested in an emotional attachment right now."

"All right then, what if he doesn't go for it? That's going to make continuing to work for him a little awkward, isn't it?"

She dismissed this idea with a wave of her fork. "Why wouldn't he go for it? Isn't casual, noncommitted sex on a regular basis with an attractive woman every man's fantasy?"

"He could still say no. Men do, for whatever reason."

She shook her head. "He won't." Sometimes when she looked at him she was struck by the sadness that seemed to weigh him down. "I think he's really lonely." She shrugged off the melancholy image of Nick and reached for another chip. "I think I'm just what Nick needs in his life right now."

"Maybe. But you need to be careful."

Familiar advice that she'd long ago grown tired of. "I've spent my whole life being careful and it taught me one thing."

"What's that?" Candace continued to look worried.

Lexie smiled, and enjoyed the thrill that filled her at the thought of her own daring. "I've learned that caution is really overrated."

After all, caution hadn't saved her from almost dying in that car wreck. It hadn't gotten her through rehab or into a new job. Playing it safe wasn't going to get her Nick Delaney, either. For that she'd have to tell caution to take a hike while she mustered up all the daring she could manage. But she had no doubt a hot guy like Nick would be worth taking a few chances for.

WHEN NICK HAD HIRED Lexie they had agreed she would work until five o'clock. He usually stayed at least until six, sometimes later. He told himself he needed the time to catch up on paperwork, but the truth was he delayed going back to his apartment as long as possible. There was nothing at home to hold his interest and a man could spend only so many evenings watching TV and eating take-out before he snapped. Sometimes he stopped by a bar, but he'd never been a big drinker, and more often than not the cheerful crowds only underscored his solitude.

So he was both surprised and pleased when Lexie lingered at the office at the end of her second week of employment. "Are you busy?" she asked, standing in the doorway between their two work spaces.

He shook his head and pushed aside the report he'd been writing for a skip-trace firm that had subcontracted some work to him. Locating people who'd skipped out on bills and other obligations was tedious, but fairly lucrative. "I figured you'd be out of here by now. Off to class or something. Or maybe a date." He couldn't imagine a woman like Lexie spending many Friday nights alone.

She shook her head and moved into the room. "No class tonight. No date, either." She glanced at him, seeming almost shy. "Can I talk to you about something?"

"Sure." He ignored the cold feeling in the pit of his stomach that rose at her words. This was it. She was leaving him already. He couldn't blame her. The job had been anything but exciting so far, and her paycheck was a third less than what she'd brought home from her previous employment. Still, he was going to miss her.

She sat in his client's chair, crossed her legs and smoothed the skirt of her tropical print dress over her knees. She wore a red scarf today, the ends tied in a small bow on the left side of her neck.

"What did you want to talk about?" he prompted.

"I have a proposition for you."

A proposition. The word set him on alert. Most of the propositions he'd encountered had been shady deals. "What is it?"

"Well…you and I seem to get along great."

"Yes." She wasn't a hard woman to like.

"And I find you very attractive."

"You do?" He'd thought he was past the point where such praise flattered him, but obviously he was wrong.

She smiled, the warmth in the look stoking a fire inside him. "Of course. And I believe you're somewhat attracted to me as well."

He didn't say anything. He couldn't deny it but he wasn't ready to reveal too much, either.

She shifted in the chair and smoothed her skirt again. He fought back a smile. It was different seeing her so…

unsettled. She generally had more self-confidence than most women he'd met. "Do you remember I told you about the list I'd made? The list of one hundred things I intend to do?"

He nodded. He'd glimpsed the little red notebook poking out of the top of her purse a time or two and had wondered what was in it. "How many things have you done so far?"

"Only about five, but I'm working on the others." She gave him a coy look. "I thought maybe you could help me with one of the items on my list."

Oh yeah? "What's that?"

"I think you and I would do well together as lovers."

He blinked. Was his horny imagination getting the better of him? "Did you say what I think you said?"

"Yes. What do you think?"

He shook his head. "No. Not a good idea."

"Why not?"

He cringed at the hurt in her eyes, and tried to soften the rejection. "It's not that I don't find you attractive. I do. But we have to work together every day. Adding sex to the equation isn't a good idea."

She lifted her chin, defiant. "I think you're wrong. I can be a professional and do my job during the day and sleep with you at night. People do it all the time."

Really? Was she that experienced with situations like this? "I don't. Besides, I'm not exactly in the market for a relationship right now."

"I'm not talking about anything serious. Just fun and sex." She smiled. "I'm not ready to get serious about anyone, either, which is the reason I picked you. And it would only be for a few months—no more than six."

He should have ended the discussion already, but her determination intrigued him. And what man wouldn't be turned on by the idea that a woman wanted him that much? "Why is that?"

"In six months I plan to take an extended trip to Spain."

"Another item on your list?"

"Yes. But I promise to find someone to take over my job here before I go, so you don't have to worry about that."

A relationship with a built-in expiration date. The idea was absurd, yet at the same time, held a certain appeal. He studied her a long moment, as if by staring at her enough, he'd figure out what was really going on inside that gorgeous head. "I didn't think women thought that way," he said.

"Thought what way?"

"About casual sex and temporary relationships. I thought those were male fantasies, while women were all about hearts and flowers and settling down."

"Some women, maybe. Even me at some point in my life."

"But not now?"

She shook her head. "I have too many things I want to do, things to learn and accomplish, places to see, people to meet. I can't do all that if I'm tied to a relationship."

Right. She made it sound so simple, but he couldn't believe intimacy between two people was ever that simple. "I'm flattered," he said. "But I still say no."

Her expression clouded. "You're not attracted to me?"

"I told you I am. Very." He leaned toward her, eyes locked to hers, telegraphing just how strong the attraction was, how much he *wanted* her. Her pupils were dilated, her lips slightly parted like a woman overtaken by passion.

At that moment it was all he could do not to clear his desk and start removing all their clothes. "A man would have to be dead not to be attracted to you," he said, his voice low. "Last time I checked I still had a pulse."

"Th-then what's wrong?" she stammered.

What *was* wrong? He blinked, trying to remember his objection to her absurd proposition. He took a deep breath, but all that did was fill his head with the scent of her, flowery and feminine and setting off sparks along every primitive pathway between his brain and his sex organs. His body, at least, had already made up his mind about Lexie.

He tore his gaze away from hers and summoned his old willpower. Reasoning returned as his head cleared. "I've always had a policy of not mixing business with pleasure," he said. "I don't see any reason to back off from that now." He almost winced. He sounded like some old coot with a steel rod for a backbone.

Instead of being angry, she looked amused. Superior. As if she knew how much he was bluffing. "Didn't you ever hear 'rules are made to be broken'?"

"Not by me. Not now."

"Why not?"

"Because I said so." Now he was channeling his father. He gripped the armrests of his desk chair and tried again. "Look. One of the things this job and my years as a cop have shown me is how screwed up life gets when people take too many chances and risk too many complications. They start out thinking they can handle it—one more hot check will take care of everything. One more time fudging on the books and they'll be out of it. One more drink and they'll stop. The next thing they know, they're in too deep."

Her expression told him she wasn't buying it. "We're

not talking embezzlement or bank robbery here. We're talking about two intelligent, healthy, single adults who are attracted to one another getting together to have a good time." She leaned toward him, her voice low and breathy. "When was the last time you had a *really* good time?"

Words stuck in his throat. His pulse pounded at his temples and in his groin. He was close to giving in. Too close.

He pulled himself away from the edge, shoving his chair back and standing, putting some distance between them. "It doesn't matter. I have a business to run and I can't be distracted."

He waited for anger, or even tears, but she surprised him by smiling—not the warm welcoming look he'd seen so many times before, but a slyer, knowing expression. She rose and looked him up and down. "All right, Nick. You've made up your mind and I respect that. For now." She turned and moved to the door.

Fear that this might be the last time he saw her gripped him. "Wait," he called. "Will you be in Monday morning?"

She looked over her shoulder at him, that same self-assured smile still in place. "I'll be here. And just so you know, I'll be making every effort to convince you to change your mind."

He swallowed hard. "You don't need to do that."

"Oh, but I do." The smile broadened. "Six months is a long time, Nick. I hate to think of spending all that time alone, don't you?"

When she was gone, he sank into his chair, the strength in his legs deserting him. He was breathing hard, as if he'd just run up four flights of stairs, and his head was spinning. So much for his blasted self-control. He'd attempted to lay down the law and all he'd done was wave a red flag in front of her. Now she was determined to change his mind.

What man stood a chance against a determined woman like Lexie Foster?

3

NICK TOLD HIMSELF he'd turned down the promise of a temporary affair in the interest of keeping a good assistant, which in his previous experience, had always been more difficult to find. But as he worked side by side with Lexie during the following week he wondered at the wisdom of his decision.

She was still an excellent assistant, charming his clients and keeping the office running smoothly. But now, in addition to lusting after her in silence, he was constantly reminded of what could be his if he could only ignore common sense and convention. The struggle made him irritable and surly, which she pretended not to notice.

Instead, she smiled and made pleasant, intelligent conversation. She continued to dress in a variety of professional yet stunning outfits. Each seemed to have been designed expressly to call his attention to her shapely curves and long legs, all topped off by a silky scarf tied around her neck, like the ribbon on a package, tempting him to unwrap her.

She made no mention of their conversation that Friday afternoon, but he was aware of her watching him—studying him, really—as if she were formulating a plan of attack.

And was it his imagination, or her ingenuity, that led

to the most innocent activities taking on a sexual connotation? Was it necessary for her to lean quite so far over his desk when she delivered letters for his signature? Had she meant for him to see the erotic black satin and lace lingerie peeking out of the bag she left in the restroom after a lunchtime shopping trip?

And speaking of lunch, he couldn't believe mere coincidence had led her to return from lunch with an ice-cream cone, which she proceeded to consume in full view of his office, her tongue slowly encircling the cone, her lips making gentle sucking noises until, in agony, he'd gotten up from his desk and slammed the door.

Today it was lipstick. When he came out of his office at midmorning she was sitting at her desk applying lipstick. Slowly. The tube caressed her lips and stained them berry-pink. Who had decided women's lipstick should have such a definitely phallic shape?

"I hate to interrupt your toilette, but I need you to call the Magnolia Hotel and make reservations for me for tonight."

She slowly twisted the lipstick back into its tube and tucked it in her purse. "The Wittier investigation certainly has you out of sorts, doesn't it?"

If she wanted to think he was feeling this way because of Stan Wittier and his wife, let her. The case certainly was contributing to his frustration. He'd followed Ellen Wittier all over town for a week and come up with absolutely nothing. If she was meeting another man she was being incredibly discreet about it.

"Tell the hotel I'd like a room on the west side of the fourteenth floor. Preferably either 1422 or 1424."

"Why those particular rooms?" she asked as she flipped through the yellow pages.

"Those rooms look directly onto the Wittiers' loft. Stan Wittier told me he's going to be out of town on business for a few days, so I figure his wife will use the opportunity to meet her lover. When she does, I'll be watching."

"What if she draws the curtains? You won't see anything."

"No curtains. I already checked. They apparently hired a decorator who's into minimalism. Or they don't want to block the view they paid big bucks for."

She found the number for the hotel and put her finger on the page to mark the spot. "Who is this boyfriend of hers, do you know?"

He shook his head. "I haven't seen a sign of him. So far, Ellen Wittier has lived a stupefyingly dull life that seems to consist mainly of shopping, having lunch with friends and attending various beauty appointments."

"I don't think she's cheating at all," Lexie said. "I think her husband's paranoid because he married a pretty young thing and doesn't spend enough time with her."

"If she's not cheating, it will be the first time in my experience that a client's been wrong about something like this. By the time somebody hires me to get the evidence, they already have a good idea what's going on."

"There's a first time for everything." She picked up the phone. "Any preference as to what kind of room? Double-double? King?"

"I don't care as long as it gives me a good view of that loft."

She looked him up and down, her gaze traveling over him deliberately. He felt his temperature rise when her vision focused on his crotch and she smiled. "I think you're more of a king-size man," she said, and punched in the number.

He turned and retreated to his office. It was either that

or snatch the phone out of her hand and do all the things to her he'd been dreaming about. Fantasies of Lexie were keeping him awake nights anyway.

Every day that passed, he was having more trouble remembering why those fantasies couldn't come true. Logic was apparently the first thing to go when the sex drive started running the show.

LEXIE HUMMED ALONG with pseudo-pop hits and waited for the hotel reservations agent to come on the line. Nick's gruffness didn't fool her one bit. She knew she'd shaken him up with her suggestion they become lovers. Though he'd done his best to keep his distance from her this week, she sensed he was weakening.

Who wouldn't melt a little in the heat of the attraction that crackled between them? Her senses stayed on hyper-alert whenever they were in the room together and when they accidentally brushed against each other it was all she could do not to moan. Ever since she'd conceived the idea of taking him as her lover she'd been able to think of little else, like a woman stranded on a desert island in need of a chocolate fix.

If Nick were chocolate, he'd be the most expensive, darkest kind, sinfully rich and sweet, with a hint of bitterness.

Now that she'd set her sights on him, no other man would do. She'd been patient so far, reminding him at every opportunity of what he was missing. But so far he hadn't taken the bait. Maybe it was time for more drastic action.

"Hello, reservations. How may I help you?"

She started as a man's voice replaced the music. "I'd like to reserve a room for tonight." She explained Nick's requirements and was assured that room 1422 was available, and that it had a king bed.

"Will there be anything else?"

She smiled, struck by a brilliant idea. If Nick wouldn't come to her, she'd simply have to go to him. After all, it would be a shame to let that king-size bed go to waste. "Yes, could I go ahead and order dinner for two to be sent up? Say, about seven o'clock? Something simple—steak and baked potatoes, with a nice salad and a good bottle of merlot."

"Very well. Is there anything else?"

"No. That's all for now. Thank you." She gave the rest of the reservation information and hung up. Good thing she'd bought that new lingerie earlier in the week. Tonight she'd put it to good use. She and Nick would enjoy a good steak dinner together and then...on to dessert.

NICK STOOD TO ONE SIDE of the window that took up most of a wall in his room at the Magnolia, binoculars trained on the loft apartment slightly below and to his right. In the three hours since Ellen Wittier had arrived home and he had checked into the hotel she'd changed into a sexy, expensive looking pair of lounging pajamas and had set the table with china and candles for what looked to be a romantic dinner.

When she'd leaned over and lit the candles, Nick's heart had sped up. He knew it! Once again, his instincts had been right. With her husband safely away at a convention in Reno, Ellen was making her move.

But now, almost an hour later, he wondered at her lover's tardiness. The candles were dripping wax on the tablecloth and Ellen was on her second glass of wine. Why was her Romeo keeping her waiting?

A knock on the door roused him from his musings. He glanced at the door, then at the clock—six forty-five.

He wasn't expecting anyone, so it was probably someone with the wrong room. He turned back to the window and raised the binoculars again.

"Nick, open up. It's me, Lexie."

Frowning, he laid aside the binoculars and went to check the door. Sure enough, Lexie was standing in the hall, looking up at the peephole, her face distorted by the fish-eye lens. He undid the locks and opened the door. "What are you doing here?" he asked.

"I came to see you." She moved past him into the room, and set her purse on the bedside table. "Nice room," she said, looking around.

"I don't have time to visit," he said. "I'm working."

She walked to the window and looked out. "Which one is the Wittiers' loft?"

"Top floor on the right." He came to stand behind her and put his hands on her shoulders. She was wearing a halter dress made of some clingy red material. Her shoulders were bare, her skin soft and warm. He ignored the tightening in his groin when he touched her. "Move back from the window a little. I don't want her to see us."

She did as he asked, colliding with him as she stepped back, sending shock waves of awareness through him. She leaned her head back and her hair brushed against his face, filling his nose with the scent of flowers.

He released her and quickly moved away. "Why are you here?" he asked again.

She walked to the bed and sat, crossing her legs. The skirt of her dress was slit at the side, revealing a long expanse of thigh. "I kept thinking of you up here, all alone, with this king-size bed." She smoothed her hand along the bedspread.

He looked away, breathing heavy. Seeing her sitting on the bed this way was only a short leap from imagining her stretched out on it. Naked. "I'm working," he said again. He was repeating himself, but his brain couldn't manage more, considering most of his blood had flowed south.

"Has anything interesting happened yet?"

Other than you showing up here like this? He shook his head. "She came home, changed into a sexy outfit, set the stage for a romantic dinner and poured the wine, but so far her lover's failed to show."

She stood and went to the window again, careful this time to keep back. "Maybe she's not waiting on anyone. Maybe she's just entertaining herself."

"Check again. There are two places set at the table."

She wrinkled her nose. "Right." She turned away from the window. "Any idea who she's meeting?"

He shook his head. "Her husband didn't know, either."

Another knock on the door interrupted him. So much for laying low. "Who is it?" he called.

"Room service."

"I didn't order any—"

"I ordered it." Lexie hurried to the door.

A waiter wheeled in a table topped with covered dishes, a vase of flowers, a bottle of wine and two glasses. "Would you like me to open the wine?" he asked.

"Yes, please," Lexie said. While he did that, she checked under the metal covers. Steam rose from the plates and the aroma of grilled steaks made Nick's mouth water.

She signed for the meal, then closed the door behind the waiter. When they were alone again, she turned to Nick. "I thought you might be hungry," she said.

She flicked her tongue along her bottom lip, reminding him of all the things he was hungry for. He checked on Ellen Wittier again, trying to compose himself. She was pouring her third glass of wine, slumped at the table, watching the candles drip.

"Come sit down," Lexie beckoned him. "Have some wine."

He sat in the desk chair, but she perched on the edge of the bed, the light from the lamp mounted on the headboard spotlighting her. The neck of her dress was low, revealing the swell of her breasts. When she leaned forward to remove the covers from the plates, he had a tantalizing glimpse of one shadowed nipple. He immediately grew hard, and hurried to spread the napkin across his lap to hide his arousal.

The steak was tender and juicy, but he scarcely tasted it, too distracted by his dinner companion.

"Where is Mr. Wittier this weekend?" she asked halfway through the meal.

"Reno. At a convention. According to the schedule he gave me he was originally supposed to fly home tonight, but he sent word yesterday that his plans had changed and he intended to stay over."

"And that's when you decided to book this room?"

He nodded. "I knew his wife wouldn't pass up the chance to spend a whole night with her lover."

"As far as you know, she's never spent any time with this phantom lover."

"I haven't seen him yet, but that doesn't mean he doesn't exist. Who else is she dressing up for tonight?"

She glanced toward the window. "He's not a very considerate lover, standing her up this way."

"Maybe he's cheating on his wife and couldn't get away."

She frowned. "You think he's married?"

"It happens. All the time."

"I suppose this job gives you a pretty jaded view of relationships between men and women, doesn't it?"

"I prefer to think of it as realistic."

"Don't you believe two people can be happy together without hurting each other?"

"I wouldn't say I didn't believe it. I just haven't known it to happen often. 'Happily-ever-after' occurs in fiction a lot more than in real life."

"What about 'happy-for-right-now'?" She laid aside her fork and looked at him. "What about two people enjoying each other for the moment and not worrying about what might happen a few months or even a few weeks from now?"

He took a long drink of wine, weighing his answer. He knew what she was getting at. Here, in this intimate setting, with Lexie so warm and willing and only inches from him, and another woman in the building across the way, alone and crying without her husband or her lover to comfort her, all of his old arguments about working together or not working together didn't seem to matter. Tonight, those objections were reduced to one question: Did he want to spend another night alone?

No, he didn't. He wanted to welcome this woman, whom he'd been lusting after for weeks, into his arms and his bed.

He pushed the table away and stood, looming over her. She tilted her head back and met his gaze. "You know I want you," he said.

"Then I'm yours," she said, and opened her arms wide.

WHEN NICK TOOK LEXIE into his arms, she sighed with joy and relief. All these weeks she'd been waiting for this. All those months in physical therapy when she'd worked so hard to get well, this was what she'd been working for, though she hadn't even known it at the time. She'd been waiting for strong arms to reach around her, for warm lips to find hers, for hands to caress her, and for the rush of blood and heat that was like a shout within her. She was alive and whole again. All that struggle and pain had been worth it to get to this moment.

She stood on tiptoe, arms reaching around him, pressing her body close to his. She felt his arousal against her belly and a thrill of anticipation surged through her, followed by a tremor of nervousness. It had been a long time since she'd had sex with a man.

He slid his hands up to cradle her head, his fingers buried in her hair, turning her face more fully to his. His lips claimed hers in a drugging kiss that she felt all the way to her toes. Long-dormant sensations came back to her, reminding her that sex was not something to be learned over and over again, but a pleasure to be enjoyed and continually perfected.

He fumbled with the fastening of her dress, and she reached back to help him. "I should probably be more patient and take it slower," he said. "But I've been imagining you naked so long I can't wait anymore to see the real thing."

She laughed and undid the button at the neck of the dress, letting the two halves of the top fall forward to hang at her waist. "I could say the same thing about you," she said.

She reached for the waistband of his pants, but he stepped back. "I want to look at you," he said. "All of you."

Feeling only a little self-conscious, she reached back and lowered the zipper of the dress, then slid it down over her hips. Clad only in pink silk bikini panties, red scarf and red stilettos, she faced him.

The reverent look in his eyes was almost her undoing. The mixture of raw lust and unabashed need send a rush of wet heat to her sex. Her breasts felt heavy and aching beneath his gaze, and her nipples rose in points anticipating his touch.

When she thought she couldn't bear another second apart from him, he moved toward her. She let out a sigh of relief, which turned to a moan when he moved past her, to the window. He checked the loft again, then drew the heavy inner drapes, closing them off from the world.

"What is she doing?" she asked.

"The lights are off in the dining room. She's in the bedroom, on the bed." He turned to her, his face pinched with some undecipherable emotion. "I think she's crying."

She felt a pang of sympathy for the lonely woman across the way, but had little time to dwell on this. With remarkable swiftness, Nick shed his clothes and moved toward her again, his erection stiff and proud, swaying with each stride.

Then he was gathering in his arms, maneuvering her toward the bed. When the back of her legs came in contact with the spread she let herself fall back.

Nick followed, and stretched out beside her, his hand on her stomach, preserving the connection. "You're more gorgeous than I imagined." He grinned. "But not naked enough."

She watched, amused, as he slipped to the floor and knelt to unfasten her shoes. She started to make a joke about him bowing before her, but all words fled as he pulled off one high heel and drew her toe into his mouth.

She moaned at the sensation of his tongue, hot and wet against her toes, touching some primitive part of her. Was it possible to come from having one's toes sucked?

From her toes, he moved to her ankles, up her calves, her knees, to her thighs, his tongue and lips finding sensitive nerves she hadn't known existed. She felt hot everywhere he touched; little flames of sensation lit the length of her body.

He hooked his thumbs underneath the sides of her panties and drew them down. She raised her hips to help him and then she was naked.

She waited, tensed, anticipating his lips on her. She could hear him breathing hard, sense his gaze on her. When she raised her head to look, he was staring at her, a half smile on his lips.

Why had he stopped? "Is—is something wrong?" she asked.

"No. Nothing's wrong. I'm just undressing you. Almost done."

He reached for the scarf at her throat, but she caught his wrist and stopped him. She'd revealed enough tonight; she wasn't ready for more. "Leave the scarf on," she said.

He looked puzzled. "Why?"

"Just…leave it on."

She waited for him to ask why, the heat of the moment already receding as she struggled to come up with a superficial explanation.

But he didn't ask for one. He simply lowered his hand to her side and his mouth to her stomach, and began working his way up her body, one kiss at a time.

She fell back again, abandoning herself once more to sensation. It was as if her body were waking from the coma all over again, nerves she'd forgotten coming to life beneath his exploring lips and tongue.

When he reached her breasts, she could stay still no longer. She arched to him, hips thrusting, silently pleading for release from this incredible, exquisite tension. She felt him smile against her, then he sucked her nipple into his mouth and she gasped with pleasure.

Her pulse beat hard against her temple, and her vision clouded as he suckled and teased, first one breast, then the other. She put her arms around him, holding on as if to an anchor. Anything to keep her from flying off the bed and soaring to the ceiling. Or breaking into pieces. Any minute now she felt she could explode, nerves stretched beyond bearing.

"Niiiick." His name was a low moan on her lips, both endearment and plea. She couldn't wait anymore. She couldn't.

He moved away from her momentarily and she lay still, eyes closed, breathing heavily. If she just had a moment to recover, she'd be ready to offer him as much pleasure as he was giving her. Just a moment…

His mouth closed around her sex, hot and wet and insistent. In that moment she shattered, light and heat rushing through her, a shout torn from her throat. Part of her really was up near the ceiling, separated from her physical body and flying on sheer pleasure. She'd forgotten how wonderful this felt. Or had it ever really felt this good before?

Nick held her as the aftermath of her climax shuddered through her, the awareness of his strong arms around her gradually bringing her back to earth. He was there when she opened her eyes, watching her with concern in his eyes. She grinned, and somehow found her voice. "Wow.

If that was the opening act, I can't wait to see the main attraction."

"Coming right up." He knelt between her legs, gently urging her thighs farther apart to accommodate him. "Pun intended."

She laughed, giddy with happiness, aware that at any moment she might burst into giggles. Not very seductresslike but she couldn't help herself. She imagined running down the halls, shouting *I'm alive. I'm alive. And it's wonderful!*

"I can't believe I was so stupid!"

His words, and the groan that followed pulled her back to the moment.

"What's wrong?"

He made a face and looked at the bedside phone. "Do you think room service would send up a condom?"

4

THERE WAS A TIME when Nick would have considered protection just another tool in his cache of supplies, but he'd gotten out of the habit since his marriage. Perhaps he was pickier, but spontaneous seduction wasn't part of his life these days.

"I have some in my purse," Lexie said.

"Some?" He arched one eyebrow in his best man-about-town imitation. The idea of her deliberately setting out to seduce him was a huge turn-on. He was a man used to doing the pursuing. The chance to be on the receiving end for a change held a wicked fascination.

She flushed. "I wanted to be prepared."

He started to get up, but she pushed him back down, and went to retrieve her purse from the table. He lay back and watched her, admiring the way her breasts swayed as she walked. She was gorgeous. Amazing.

Her boldness had taken him by surprise at first, but once they were both naked, he sensed this wasn't an everyday thing with her. She'd been as eager and needy as him, and it had been all he could do to force himself to take it slow, to make this good for her. He wouldn't let her think he was the kind of man to take his own pleasure first and leave her wanting more.

And then she'd come, her cries pushing him to the brink of his own desire. Just as well he had this moment to pull back, or else everything would be over before they'd really started.

She returned and crawled back into the bed, the ends of the scarf trailing over her breast, the cherry-red silk bright against her almond-colored skin. Why had she insisted on wearing the scarf? What was she hiding under there?

Did she really think anything he might see would make a difference to him? Later, he'd talk to her about it, but now was not the time to argue.

He reached out to take the condom, but she pushed aside his hand. "Allow me."

She tore open the packet and leaned over him, the scarf brushing the sensitive head of his penis. He sucked his breath through his teeth, willing himself to stay in control.

Then her hands were around him, cool and soft, squeezing gently as she slowly rolled the condom on. He felt himself pulse against her palm, and closed his eyes, reveling in the sensation but fighting against it, too. She was torturing him. But what sweet torture.

She straddled him, her calves cool and sleek against his thighs. Then she slid over him, surrounding him with her heat and wetness. He clasped her hips as she began to ride him, matching her rhythm, every movement sending shock waves of feeling through him.

He opened his eyes and watched her, her breasts bouncing with each thrust, her eyes half-closed, her mouth slightly open, cheeks flushed. He moved his hands up to caress her breasts, and smiled as she gasped in obvious pleasure.

She planted her palms on his chest and adjusted the tilt

of her hips to a more acute angle. He moaned and his vision clouded. He couldn't hold back any longer.

His climax slammed into him, stealing breath and sense and leaving him weak as a baby. He put his arms around her and pulled her close, pressing his face against her breasts, dimly aware that she was coming again, tensing around him then releasing. She leaned into him, collapsing into his arms.

They lay like that for a long while, fused together by passion. She was all softness and heat, smelling of flowers, her breath a warm tickle against his ear.

It had been a long time since he'd held a woman like this. He'd forgotten how good it felt. How right.

The thought jolted out of his haze. Where had that idea come from? This wasn't a matter of right and wrong, only a moment of physical pleasure.

Yet he was reluctant to let her go. In fact, she was the first to pull away. She gave him a sleepy-eyed smile, kissed the corner of his mouth, then got up and padded into the bathroom.

While she was gone, he disposed of the condom, then dragged himself over to the window to check on Ellen Wittier again. Her rooms were dark. She must have gone to bed. Alone, from the look of things; a night-light in the hallway cast a faint glow over the still untouched dinner for two laid out on the dining room table.

He let the curtains fall back into place and crawled under the covers, trying to sort out what had just happened between him and Lexie. It was as if he'd lost himself for a moment, become some other person. A person who needed Lexie in his life.

A dangerous thought.

She came out of the bathroom and slipped under the covers beside him. He opened his arms to her, welcoming her to his side even as part of his brain screamed that he ought to keep some distance. He didn't have room in his life for the feelings she conjured in him, this tenderness and wanting.

The thought kept him awake long after she was sleeping soundly, her head still on his shoulder, her body shaped to his. The scent of her surrounded him—floral perfume and female musk, so sweet and intoxicating. Only his growing uneasiness drove him to slip from beneath her, out of the bed.

He dressed as quickly as he could, watching her as he did so. He thought about leaving a note, but what would he say? He hoped she understood he wasn't running away from her. Actually, he was, but he needed time to think, time to gain perspective and put the night in its proper place.

He left, shutting the door behind him, hearing the tumblers of the lock fall into place. If only it were as easy to lock away emotions and feelings and all the messy things that got in the way of a sane, uncomplicated life.

WHEN LEXIE AWOKE she sensed she was alone even before she opened her eyes. The room was too quiet, the only sounds were her own breathing and the muted hum of the air-conditioning unit. She rolled over in bed and stared at the empty space beside her. The pillow still bore the indentation from Nick's head but when she reached out to touch it the space was cold. He'd been gone for a while.

She couldn't say she was surprised. Though he'd been an intense, passionate lover she'd had a sense that he was holding something back. While his body had been fully engaged in their lovemaking, some part of his personality had remained aloof.

She could dismiss some of that as typical male behavior, and perhaps a portion was due to the cautious nature of a former policeman. But intuition told her there was more to Nick than a former cop wanting to keep things superficial. She wasn't sure what exactly was going on with him, but she looked forward to the chance to find out.

She sat up and stretched, relishing the slight soreness that reminded her she had been well and truly sated the night before. Her boldness with Nick had paid big dividends. She smoothed her palms along her ribs, smiling at the memory of his hands on her.

He'd been right about one thing; last night had changed the situation between them. She had no doubt she could continue to be a professional assistant to him, but now there would be an increased awareness between them. Every interaction would have an extra edge, and even as she went about the mundane tasks of her job, she'd be anticipating when they would be together again.

And they would be together again. No way was she going to pass up a chance to enjoy another night like the last one.

Still smiling, she reached for her clothes and began to dress. She'd promised Nick six months before she left for Spain and other adventures. In the meantime, he was just the man to help her complete some of the more *adventurous* items on her list.

She laughed. Oh yes, she and Nick were going to have a *very* good time together.

NICK SPENT A GOOD PART of the weekend parked near Ellen Wittier's condo, waiting for her mystery lover to appear.

But from his vantage point he saw only Ellen by herself: talking on the phone, watching television or eating a solitary meal. Stan Wittier returned Sunday evening from his convention and all appeared well.

Maybe Lexie was right. Maybe the woman wasn't cheating on her husband. He supposed it happened, that there were still married people who were faithful to each other. He just hadn't had the opportunity to meet many of them in his two careers.

He'd told himself he wasn't going to think about Lexie, but he might as well try to stop breathing. How could he not think about the woman when he could still feel her imprint on his body, still smell her scent on his hands? Every time he closed his eyes his brain insisted on throwing up the image of her naked, an erotic movie playing out against his eyelids.

Which meant he'd spent half the weekend with a hard-on and the other half annoyed with himself for getting so caught up with a woman that he let her distract him from his work. He was almost grateful when Monday morning arrived with its promise of mundane routine.

Except, of course, that Monday also meant facing Lexie again. He braced himself for her wrath. In his experience, women didn't appreciate it when you walked out on them without so much as a note the way he had. They didn't seem to understand that sometimes it was better not to say anything than to risk putting the wrong thing in writing. At least then you had less chance of your words being used against you.

"Good morning, Nick." She looked up from her desk when he arrived, her voice cheerful, her ruby-tinted lips curved up in a smile. The sight of her, dressed in a clingy red top that dipped low in the front to show off an enticing glimpse of cleavage, sent a jolt through him. Apparently Lexie clothed could arouse him as much as the memory of her naked.

"Good morning." He nodded to her, trying to act casual, trying to avoid staring.

"Did you have a good weekend?" she asked.

Was this a trick question? Was she waiting for him to bring up the events that had started off the weekend? Did she expect him to admit she'd shaken him up, and not in a good way?

"It was fine." He threw the conversational ball back to her. "How was yours?"

She assumed a coy expression, her eyes sparkling with teasing mirth. "Oh, I had a *very* nice weekend. There's nothing like fantastic sex to get things off to a good start."

That she'd thought the sex they'd enjoyed was fantastic pleased him. Apparently he hadn't lost his touch.

But then something black and ugly wrapped itself around him. She had been talking about the two of them, hadn't she? "So what did you do this weekend?" he asked casually. "I mean, after Friday?"

"Oh, I went shopping. To the movies. Fun stuff."

Alone, he hoped, then pushed back the thought. He didn't have any right to tell her who to see or what to do with her time. One night didn't give him any claim to her.

On this depressing note, he went into his office and shut the door. He focused on catching up on paperwork, and tried to forget all about the woman on the other side of the door.

But the woman apparently wasn't going to let herself be forgotten. He'd scarcely pulled the first file from the stack on the corner of his desk when she came breezing into his office without even knocking. He looked up, annoyed. "Yes?"

"How did you spend your weekend?" she asked.

Here it was then. She wasn't going to let it go until she'd wrung some kind of apology from him for running out on her. He frowned. "I really don't have time to discuss this right now," he began.

She sat in the chair across from his desk and crossed her legs, a good bit of knee and shapely thigh, clad in sheer black stockings, showing beneath the hiked-up hem of her black skirt. Did she do that deliberately, knowing the move commanded his attention?

"I know what you were doing," she said. "You were watching Ellen Wittier. Did you find anything? Did her lover ever show?"

He shook his head. "No sign of the guy."

"I've been thinking about this and I think you should let me talk to her."

He shook his head. "No way. I don't want her to get suspicious."

"She won't be suspicious." She leaned toward him. "You said yourself she spends a lot of time alone. So she's probably lonely. And lonely women like to talk. I'll simply arrange to run into her somewhere and strike up a conversation."

"Right. And she's going to tell you—a stranger—all about her boyfriend?"

"I won't be a stranger by the time we've talked a few minutes." Her smile would have looked smug on anyone else. On her it was flat-out sexy. Confident. The smile of a woman who'd seen you naked and knew exactly what to do to make you beg.

Not that she'd made him beg, but it was a tempting fantasy….

He pulled his mind out of that trap and focused on business. The truth was, he wasn't getting anywhere with this case on his own. And Lexie's idea made a certain amount of sense. "All right. You can give it a try. But be careful. Don't give anything away."

"I won't. Now didn't you say you had her schedule?"

He opened a drawer and took out the case file. In it were the copies of Ellen's date book that Wittier had given Nick. He handed the sheets to Lexie.

She scanned the pages, then tapped a pink-painted nail against one. "This is great. She has an appointment for a manicure at a nail salon in LoDo. I'll make an appointment for the same time and it'll be easy to strike up a conversation."

He nodded and replaced the sheets in the file. "Let's hope you find something."

"Or maybe I'll find out she really *isn't* cheating. Our client ought to be happy with that."

So it was "our" client now? He really couldn't object to that. If she wanted to help out with a few investigations, he'd let her. But he'd make the rules about when and where. As long as he remained in charge, everything would be okay.

She stood and smoothed her skirt. "I'll call and make an appointment at the nail salon right away."

She turned to leave but he cleared his throat, stopping her. "Was there something else?" she asked.

"Uh, yeah." His chest was tight. He hated this kind of thing but he wasn't going to be a jerk about this. "About Friday night…"

He'd half hoped she'd jump in with another comment

about how "fantastic" it had been, saving him from having to grovel, but no such luck. She fixed him with a level gaze and waited.

"Sorry I ran out like that," he said. "Without a note. I—" He shrugged. "I'm not much for notes."

"It's okay," she said. "About the note. Not that you left."

Right. So she did think he was a jerk. He waited for her to let him have it, but she surprised him by sitting down again and pulling her chair closer. "It would have been okay if you had stayed," she said. "I mean, I wouldn't have read more into it than you wanted." She smiled. "I just want us to have a good time. To enjoy each other for the next few months."

Something like relief rushed over him, coupled with innate caution. "I did have a good time." A great time.

"Me, too." She stood again, still smiling. "Now that we understand each other, I'll go make that appointment."

He watched her go, then collapsed back against his chair, stunned. If he were one of those hard-boiled types popular in forties' movies, he'd have a bottle of whiskey stashed in his desk for moments like this one.

Unfortunately, the only pain relievers in his desk drawer were half a bottle of aspirin and a roll of antacid. Not enough to sharpen his thinking where Lexie was concerned. *She* might think they understood each other but as far as he was concerned, there was no understanding women. Especially one like Lexie who was in turns tough and tender, who made love as if she'd never have the chance again and who hid secrets behind silk scarves.

But then, they all had secrets to hide, didn't they? Private wounds they kept hidden from the world. Maybe that was what had unnerved him most about those intimate hours at the hotel: some part of him had recognized that Lexie might be the one to uncover those wounds, the one to learn his secrets. And maybe that scared him more than anything.

5

LEXIE WAITED IN HER CAR until she saw Ellen Wittier go into the nail salon. A few moments later, she followed. A string of bells attached to the door announced her entrance. The young Vietnamese woman who was working on Ellen's nails looked up. "May I help you?" she asked.

"I have an appointment for a manicure."

The woman looked toward the back of the shop and said something in Vietnamese. Another young woman emerged from behind a beaded curtain. "You pick color," she instructed, gesturing toward a turntable filled with bottles of polish.

Lexie took her time perusing the polish, studying Ellen's reflection in the mirror behind the manicure table. She was an attractive woman, perhaps in her mid- to late-thirties, dressed in an expensive-looking silk tank dress and Jimmy Choo sandals Lexie immediately coveted. Her hair and makeup were done just so. Either Ellen was very particular about her appearance or she had nothing better to occupy her time.

"I ready for you now." The manicurist waved Lexie over to her table, next to the one where Ellen sat.

"Great." She reached for her usual pink polish, then hesitated and impulsively grabbed a bottle of bright red dubbed Hot Tomato. The new, bolder version of Lexie was definitely a hot tomato kind of gal.

"How are you today?" the manicurist asked, her words a pleasant singsong.

"Bored." She gave an exaggerated sigh and glanced toward Ellen. "I'm new in town and my husband's away so much with his business. I don't know what to do with myself."

Her attempt to draw Ellen into conversation worked. "What does your husband do?" she asked.

"He works for a software developer." A safe enough choice, since Denver was riddled with high-tech firms, despite the tech bust a few years ago. "We haven't been married all that long," she continued. "We met at a fund-raiser in Houston a few years back and were immediately attracted to each other." She shook her head. "I used to laugh at women my age who dated men old enough to be their fathers, and then it happened to me."

"I know just what you mean." Ellen managed a small smile. "My husband is fifteen years older than I am."

"Mine is almost twenty years older, but you'd never know it to look at him. I think that's what attracted me to him. He was so dynamic and sure of himself." Amazing how glibly the lies rolled off Lexie's tongue. Within a matter of seconds she'd created an elaborate fantasy for herself and her mythical spouse.

"Other hand, please."

"Oh, sure." She gave her other hand into the manicurist's care. "Of course my family thought I was crazy to marry him and move to Colorado. Some days I wonder if they weren't right. I mean, not that I don't love him—I really do. But he's gone so much and here I am." She shrugged.

"Yes, that can be difficult." Ellen turned her attention back to her manicurist. "A little rounder shape, please."

Lexie's smile faltered. So much for becoming best buddies with Ellen Wittier. She'd been polite, but no more. Lexie would have to think of another approach.

"How short you want?" The nail tech's question distracted her.

"Oh, that's fine right there. Thank you."

"You say your husband is older than you?" the tech asked.

"Yes."

"Mine is older, too." The tech nodded, then rubbed the third finger of Lexie's left hand. "You no wear ring?"

Lexie felt heat rise to her face. Damn! She'd forgotten all about a ring. "Uh, I never wear it when I have a manicure," she said. "I'm too afraid I'll take it off and then leave it behind." She chuckled, and didn't have to fake nervousness. "I'm still so new at this marriage thing." She glanced toward Ellen, who was gazing out the front window of the shop, her expression blank. "I just wish my husband could be home more."

"It is difficult when the two of you have to be apart so much." Ellen turned toward her again. "It gets a little easier after a while."

Does it? Lexie remembered the lonely woman who'd wandered the empty loft and then lain across the bed, crying on Friday night. "You sound like you might have a little experience," she said. "Does your husband travel in his work, too?"

Ellen nodded. "Yes. It gets lonely sometimes, but it's made me really appreciate the time we have together."

"I wish my husband stay away more." Lexie's nail tech

rubbed the buffing block vigorously over Lexie's nails. "He under foot all the time."

All the women laughed then. The two nail techs began speaking in rapid Vietnamese. Lexie looked at Ellen. "I'm Lexie F-Fellows. Lexie Fellows."

"Ellen Wittier."

Time to make her move. "What are you doing after you're finished here?" Lexie asked. "I mean, are you busy? Maybe we could have lunch or something."

"That would be nice."

"Great. I saw a cute little tea room around the corner. Maybe you can give me some advice on how to adjust to my situation." And just maybe she'd solve this case and show Nick how fortunate he was to have someone like her in his corner.

NICK WAS AT HIS APARTMENT making dinner—frozen pizza and beer—when the doorbell rang. He checked the clock and frowned. The only people who ever rang his bell were kids selling stuff and evangelists and neither of them were likely to be out after seven on a weeknight.

Setting aside his beer, he went to the door and looked out. His heart gave a funny jump at the sight of Lexie standing there. She was dressed more casually than usual, in khaki short shorts and a sleeveless white shirt, tied at the waist. Cute, but not a seductress outfit. Which probably meant she hadn't come over to jump his bones. More's the pity.

He opened the door. "Hey, what's up?"

"Good news. Can I come in?"

He held the door open wider. She ducked under his arm and scooted past. He looked back over his shoulder at her, enjoying the way her curvy rear end wiggled as she walked. One thing for sure, their encounter the other night had awakened a lustful side of him.

"What's going on?" he asked. He moved toward the kitchen.

She followed. "I was going to wait until you got to the office tomorrow morning, but I was too excited. I hope I'm not interrupting anything." She looked around the room, as if searching for something. Or someone.

"Right. I always dress like this when I have a hot date," he said, reclaiming his beer and taking a long drink.

She checked out his faded black basketball shorts and gray sweatshirt with the sleeves ripped out. "So I'm not interrupting anything. Good."

The timer dinged and he bent to take the pizza from the oven. "You want a beer?"

She shook her head. "No thanks."

"There's some soda in the fridge. Or you can have water, if you don't mind drinking out of the tap."

"Soda's fine." She opened the refrigerator and took out a can while he carried the pizza to the bar and pushed aside the clutter that always accumulated there: bills, address book, take-out menus, old newspapers and a pair of hand-cuffs left over from his days at HPD.

Lexie watched, practically vibrating with impatience, ready to spill her news, but he enjoyed making her wait.

He took two plates from the cabinet and gestured toward the bar. "Have a seat and help yourself to some pizza."

"No thanks. I just had dinner. Guess who with?"

He slid two large slices of pizza onto his plate and cracked open another beer. "Mick Jagger? Oprah Winfrey?"

"Come on, Nick. Be serious."

"You don't think I'm serious?" He took a huge bite of pizza and chewed, his eyes never leaving her. Even annoyed at him she was sexy as hell. Maybe *especially* when she was annoyed with him.

"I had dinner with Ellen Wittier," she said finally. "And lunch."

"Ah." He nodded and washed the pizza down with a long swig of beer. "I take it you two really hit it off."

"We did." She leaned toward him, her expression eager. "There is no way that woman is cheating on her husband."

"How do you know that?"

"She told me."

He choked on a half-chewed slice of pepperoni and went into a coughing fit. Lexie jumped up from her bar stool and pounded on his back. "You asked her?" he wheezed.

"Not in so many words. What, do you think I'm stupid?"

Not stupid. But naive. And she was completely untrained. He never should have let her get involved in a case this way. "What did you say to her?"

"I pretended to be new in town, married to an older man and lonely because he was out of town all the time."

"I get it. A kindred spirit."

"Exactly. Someone she could relate to and feel comfortable confiding in."

"And did she confide in you?"

"She did. I was right—she *is* terribly lonely. But when I suggested that a lot of women in her position might find a boyfriend, she rejected the idea immediately." Her expression softened. "She really loves him. She just feels he shuts her out too much. That he's let work be more important to him than she is."

Right. Where had he heard those words before? Was this the standard excuse now for cheating wives? "Then who was she waiting for the other night when he was out of town?"

"She was waiting for him. For Stan." She resumed her seat on the bar stool next to his. "I said something about hating to eat alone and she said what was worse was when she made dinner for both of them and her husband didn't show. She said the other night he'd promised to try to sneak away from the convention and get an early flight back from Reno. When she didn't hear from him, she assumed he was on his way home, then he never showed."

Nick chewed, considering all this. On one hand, it was a pretty lame story. On the other, why make something like that up? Whoever Ellen Wittier had made dinner for, the person definitely hadn't showed up. And he'd seen no sign at all of another man—or woman—in her life.

"If what you're saying is true, why did Stan Wittier hire me to follow his wife and gather proof of an affair? He said he was sure she was cheating."

"I don't know. Didn't you say he told you his first wife had left him for someone else?"

"Yes, and apparently his business partner's wife left him also."

"Then maybe he feels guilty about leaving her alone so much and because she's younger and very pretty, he's worried about history repeating itself."

"He feels guilty, so he's making her out to be the bad guy?" He shook his head. "Are you taking psychology courses along with Spanish?"

"Haven't you heard of self-fulfilling prophesies? People take what they fear most and end up making it come true. Maybe a man who fears his wife will cheat subconsciously does things that are more likely to lead to her infidelity."

"Like leaving her alone way too much and failing to keep dinner dates?" It made sense in a chick-logic kind of way. "So what do I tell Wittier?"

"Tell him his wife loves him and isn't cheating on him, but if he really wants to save his marriage, he needs to spend more time with her. He needs to show her she's more important to him than his job."

"I'm a detective, not a marriage counselor."

"Then tell him you didn't find anything. That's the truth."

"Maybe. Or maybe it makes me look like I'm a lousy P.I."

"Are you naturally this skeptical, or do you work at it?"

"You work the streets of Houston for a while and see how much you trust people." Add in being blindsided by a little marital infidelity of your own and who wouldn't be cynical?

"I think you're just being stubborn. You don't like to admit you were wrong about Ellen Wittier."

"Show me someone who likes to admit he's wrong and I'll show you a liar." He drained his beer can and tossed it toward the trash can. It sailed in without touching the rim. "Besides, ninety-eight percent of the time I *am* right." Maybe that sounded like arrogance to her, but it was the truth. He'd always had good instincts about his work. So they'd failed him this one time. It only proved he was human.

He got up and retrieved another beer from the refrigerator. "You sure you don't want a drink? I've got some rum." He opened a cabinet and showed her the bottle.

"Okay, I'll take some rum."

He brought it to her and she carefully poured a generous measure of liquor into her soda, then rocked the can from side to side to mix the contents. She took a sip. "Not bad."

"Where'd you learn to mix drinks like that?"

"Delta Sigma Epsilon. With that little trick you can smuggle alcohol in almost anywhere."

He might have known she'd pledged a sorority. She had that sleek, debutante look about her, but with an extra layer of maturity that appealed to him.

"Do you know Spanish?"

The question derailed the fantasy he'd been about to embark upon and brought him back to the present. "A little. I took a course for police officers once and picked up a few more things on the street. Why?"

She rested her elbows on the bar and propped her head in her hands. "It's this Spanish class I'm taking. I'm having a really hard time catching on."

"Maybe I can help you out." He held up the can of beer. *"Cerveza."*

"Cerveza," she repeated. She picked up a section of newspaper from the pile at the end of the bar. "And this."

"Periódico." He checked the section heading. *"El seccion deportivo."*

"This?" She showed him her empty glass.

"Un vaso. Come on, give me something a little more challenging."

She looked around the room, then hopped off her stool and picked up the sport coat he'd thrown over a chair. "This?"

"Chaqueta. Is that the best you can do?"

She looked around, her lips shoved out in a pout as she searched. Then she smiled, a positively devilish look in her eyes. She propped one foot on the coffee table. "All right then. What would you call my leg?"

"Beautiful. *Hermosa.* Gorgeous. *Magnifico."* He set his beer on the bar and moved toward her.

"*Gracias.* I mean what would you call a leg?"

He thought a moment, digging deeper in his memory. "*Pierna.*"

"My arm?"

"*Brazo.*"

"How about this?" She untied the knot at her waist and pushed aside the halves of the shirt to reveal her stomach.

"*El stomacho?*" He knew that wasn't right, but she bought it. He watched, holding his breath as she undid the remaining buttons.

She trailed one red-painted nail across the curve of her breast above her bra. "And what would you call this?"

He drew a blank, his mind too fogged by lust to think clearly. "*Melones.*" Actually, the word for melons. Close enough.

"How about this?" She pulled the bra down and pointed to her nipple, pink and erect.

He put his hands on her shoulders and looked down at her, breathing hard. In a minute he'd have his mouth on her and neither one of them would care what anything was called.

"Come on, what's it called." She flicked her finger across the taut peak. His cock twitched in response.

"Uh, *teton?*"

She laughed. "I think you're making that up." She reached out to cup his erection. "What's this?"

This one he knew. "*Aparato.* As in, I can't wait to use my *aparato* on you." He nuzzled her ear.

"I know you're making things up now."

"I am?" He drew her earlobe into his mouth and smiled as she gasped. He pulled back just far enough to look her in the eye. "Lesson over."

He bent to kiss her neck, but her ever-present scarf was in the way. It was buff colored satin tonight, edged in black stitching. "What's with the scarves?" he asked, taking hold of one end.

"Comes in handy if I ever need a blindfold," she quipped. Her eyes met his, a dark, shuttered look that warned him not to press her further on the subject.

Instead, he pulled her closer, his erection jutting into the softness of her belly. "Do you need to blindfold people often?"

"No. But there's a first time for everything."

Their first time had been spectacular. He was ready for a repeat. He brought his hand up to cover her breast, the nipple pressed into his palm. His mouth found hers, his kiss insistent, devouring. Her lips parted and he plunged his tongue between them. She was hot and sweet and it was all he could do not to groan with pleasure. He'd been on edge with desire almost since the moment he'd walked out of that hotel room the other day. She was like the sweetest delicacy for him—one taste was never going to be enough.

LEXIE ARCHED AGAINST HIM, angling her mouth more firmly against his. He tasted like beer, malty and slightly bitter. She didn't like to drink beer, but kissing it was a different story. Especially when the man doing the kissing was also caressing her breast, making tiny circles around her nipple with one finger, every stroke sending sparks of heat dancing across her nerve endings.

The solid thickness of his penis pressed against her stomach. She ground her hips against him, letting him know she was as eager as he was. The memory of the other night was still fresh on her skin and she couldn't wait for a repeat.

He crushed her more tightly to him, and backed her up against the bar. He bared her other breast, then lowered his head to take her nipple in his mouth. She reached back to brace herself as he teased her with his tongue. Her elbow jostled the pile of papers at the end of the bar and sent them cascading to the floor.

Something hard hit her ankles. "Ouch!"

He raised his head. "What's wrong? Was I too rough?"

"No, it's just—" She bent and retrieved the item that had hit her. A pair of handcuffs.

She laughed. "What are you doing with these?"

"I was cleaning out a bunch of junk from my cop days and these were in with some other stuff. I set them on the bar, intending to put them in the closet, and never got around to it."

She stared at the cuffs. They were thick and heavy— serious restraints, not the play cuffs she'd seen in novelty stores. The hot tension between her legs increased as she thought of all the things two people might do with a pair of handcuffs like this.

"Why are you smiling like that?" he asked.

She hadn't realized she was smiling. Her eyes met his. "Do you remember me telling you about my list?"

"The list of things you want to do with your life?" He nodded. "What about it?"

"I think I told you you could help me with some of the items on my list."

His expression grew wary. "Yeah. So?"

"So-o-o-o." She dragged the edge of the cuffs down his chest. "One of the items on my list is to have kinky sex at least once." Item number thirty-seven. She'd erased it once, then put it back. After all, the whole point of the list was to satisfy her secret desires. All of them.

He swallowed hard. "How kinky?"

She dangled the handcuffs from one finger. "Oh, I think handcuffs would be kinky enough. For now."

His eyes darkened and he pulled her close once more, his voice husky. "I think I could get into that." He kissed her temple. "I promise I'll be gentle. I won't do anything you don't want me to do."

She laughed, realizing what he was thinking. Wasn't that just like a man? "I didn't mean you handcuffing *me*." She reached down and snapped one half of the cuffs around his wrist. "I intend to handcuff *you*."

6

NICK STARED at the metal cuff snapped around his wrist, then at Lexie. "I don't think so," he said. "I'm not really into—"

She wasn't listening to him. Still with that devilish smile on her lips, she slipped one hand beneath the waistband of his shorts. The next thing he knew she quite literally had him by the balls and was leading him into the bedroom.

"Come on, Lexie, this isn't funny." His mouth was still protesting, though his body wasn't resisting at all. What did that say about him, that he'd let her subdue him with the mere touch of her hand?

She backed him up against the bed and nudged him into a sitting position. "We'd better get you out of these clothes," she said, sliding her hands up under his shirt.

Her palms were cool on his stomach, her fingers caressing his muscles, lightly playing over his nipples. She worked her way up to his shoulders, smoothly pushing the sweatshirt up over his head, teasing his cuffed hand out of the armhole opening. She smoothed her hands back down his chest. "I *do* enjoy undressing you," she said. "It's like unwrapping a very nice present."

He grunted as her hands slipped under the waistband

of his shorts, over his hips and back beneath his buttocks. He stood and she pushed the shorts to the floor, her face level with his erection, which was bobbing around like an excited kid, demanding attention. She wrapped her fingers around his shaft and trailed her tongue across his balls. "You may think you're not going to like this, but I think you're going to like it very much," she said.

"I don't think we need the handcuffs to enjoy each other." He grasped her shoulders, enjoying the view of her with her mouth on him. "I want my hands free to touch you."

"That is nice." She stood, and pressed her palms flat against his chest, pushing him down toward the bed again. "But the whole point is to help me take care of another item on my list. And I think we need the handcuffs for that."

Once again she took him by surprise, fastening the free end of the cuffs around the headboard. He craned his neck to look at the results. The wood was sturdy, but he was probably strong enough to break it. It would mean wrecking the bed, though. "You'd better get the key," he said.

"Why? We don't need it yet."

"Just get it. What if there's a fire or something?" Maybe once she had the key in her hand, he could persuade her to use it.

"All right. Where is it?"

"Top dresser drawer. Left-hand side. There's a box with tie tacks and stuff in it. The key's in there."

She retrieved the key and laid it on the nightstand. Just out of his reach. "There. But you're not going to need it yet. The only fire is going to be the one we start right here in this bed. Now stop worrying and watch me."

She slid out of her shorts and underwear, so that she was naked from the waist down. She knew what would grab his attention, didn't she? He watched as she walked to his closet, hips swaying. She opened the door and studied the contents for a moment, then returned with three of his neckties, which she used to fasten his other hand and both feet to the bed.

Now he was lying on his back, spread-eagled before her, his penis standing at attention like a flag pole. He told himself he'd break free any minute now. As soon as it stopped being interesting.

When he was firmly tied down, she slipped off her blouse and bra. Then she stood back from the bed, watching him, saying nothing.

He cleared his throat. "Didn't your mother tell you it's not polite to stare?"

"I'm not staring, I'm admiring. How do you feel?"

"I feel ridiculous." And hot, incredibly hot. Every nerve was on red alert, waiting for her to touch him. "Come here."

She shook her head. "I will in a minute. First I have to do something." She turned and left the room.

He stared after her, fighting panic. What the hell was she up to? Was she going to leave him here like this? Was this her idea of a joke?

He was attempting to pull his feet out of their restraints when she returned. "Lie still," she said, climbing up onto the bed beside him. "You'll like this, I promise."

She had a bottle in her hand. "Is that olive oil?" he asked, frowning.

"I couldn't find any massage oil, so I figured this would do."

He was going to make some comment about being

trussed up like a chicken and marinated in oil when she straddled his stomach and he all but forgot how to speak. Or breathe.

She was wet—wet and hot—where the brush of hair between her legs met his stomach. "I'll be gentle," she cooed, beginning to smooth the oil across his chest and shoulders. "I won't do anything you don't want me to do."

Her fingers kneaded and stroked, forcing the tension out of his muscles until he relaxed against the restraints and gave himself up to her touch. Right now all he wanted was for her to keep touching him. To keep the wanting building within him, and to eventually satisfy that wanting.

She rubbed oil around his nipples, then ducked her head and trailed her tongue across the spot. "How does it taste?" he managed to ask.

"Good." Her tongue flicked back and forth across his nipple. He closed his eyes and groaned.

"Might be better with a little rosemary and garlic."

She laughed and he tried to lunge for her, to make her pay for that remark, but he was helpless against his restraints. He hated the sensation, yet some part of his mind embraced the idea that there was nothing for him to do now but enjoy.

She moved down, straddling his thigh now, her hands smoothing the oil across his stomach, down between his legs and along the length of his shaft. "Easy," he croaked as her fingers tightened around him. The sensation of her skin and the warm oil had him on a thin edge.

"You can hold on a little longer, can't you?" she said. "Think about something else. Baseball statistics. Multiplication tables."

"Not a big baseball fan." He doubted if he could think

how to count just now, all his energy focused on the space between her hands.

She released her hold on him and sat back. He opened his eyes and met her gaze. Her eyes were bright, her face flushed, lips parted—the picture of a woman fully aroused.

"My turn," he said. "Untie me and I'll give you a massage."

"Thanks, but I can do that." She poured more oil into her hands and smoothed it across her breasts, massaging it into her skin, stroking her distended nipples. He watched, mesmerized, wondering how much more of this he could stand.

LEXIE WATCHED NICK through half-closed eyes, amazed at how much seeing his reaction to her was turning her on. She'd never done anything remotely this wild in her life.

Look what she'd been missing! Having Nick at her mercy like this was powerful and erotic. She could do anything and he'd be powerless to resist. But what she most wanted to do was to give him an incredible experience he'd never forget.

She leaned forward, bracing her hands on either side of his neck. "How do I taste?" she asked.

Her vision fogged as he sucked the tip of her breast into his mouth, and with every flick of his tongue she felt her pelvic muscles contract. She couldn't remember a time when she'd been so aware of every part of her physical body. After all those months of pain, it was now giving her so much pleasure.

She pulled back, unable to stand much more. "Condoms?" she gasped.

"Nightstand drawer."

She found the box—brand new from the looks of it—

and smiled. She took out a packet and started to open it, then thought better of it. "Be right back," she said, hopping off him.

"What now?" he groaned.

"Need to wash off the olive oil." She hurried to the bathroom and returned with a damp washcloth and sliver of soap. "I don't think olive oil is good with latex."

He didn't say anything, just closed his eyes and let her wash him, his face a mask of concentration. She hurried, then tossed the wet rag and soap onto the floor beside the bed and quickly sheathed him.

The nervousness she'd avoided until now caught up with her as she straddled him again. She felt foolish, up here practically on her own. She leaned back and freed his feet, unknotted the tie on one hand, then took the key from the nightstand and unfastened the cuffs.

While he was still freeing himself and flexing his fingers she guided him into her. He slid in easily, filling her completely. She tensed her thighs, clasping and holding him, savoring the feelings, the sensation of being joined to Nick in a way that went beyond the physical.

Then he grasped her hips, his fingers digging into her flesh, rocking her, urging her to meet his rhythm. "Come on," he panted, just under his breath. "Come on."

She laughed at his impatience and met him thrust for thrust, excitement building to euphoria. She wanted more, and more, and more.

When her climax hit her, she screamed, every inhibition abandoned in favor of joy. Nick slid his arms around her and pulled her close, crushing her against his chest as he followed her over the edge. She nestled her cheek in the hollow of his shoulder and marveled at the strength in the arms that held her, and the tenderness in the hands that began to stroke her back.

She'd spent a lot of time alone in the six months since her accident, and even before that had never been one to mind her own company. She'd had good times and been happy and took some satisfaction in knowing she didn't need anyone else to complete her.

But tonight with Nick had reminded her that there were some kinds of happiness you could never know on your own. Things that went beyond physical pleasure, like discovering how powerful you could be in the face of another's trust and surrender, or the satisfaction of resting with a man's strong arms around you.

She couldn't say why Nick brought out these things in her, whether it was the place she was at in her life, or the man himself.

He shifted beneath her and rolled them onto their sides until they were facing each other, still joined together. "That was pretty incredible," he said.

She grinned. "Pretty incredible."

He brushed aside a lock of hair that had fallen forward onto her cheek. "I still can't believe I let you tie me up."

"It was worth it, wasn't it?"

"Mmmm." He kissed the side of her mouth and slid out of her. "Next time it's my turn. We'll see how you like it."

"If I like it half as much as you do, I won't be sorry."

"Then you won't be sorry."

He slipped out of bed and she watched as he walked toward the bathroom. Nick definitely deserved some credit for these discoveries she was making about herself. And for all his mistrustful, sometimes prickly nature he let down his guard a little with her. She wasn't sure how much he was willing to reveal but she was willing to wait to find out.

NICK STOOD in the bathroom and tried to figure out exactly what had happened back there in the bedroom. Mind-blowing sex, obviously. An uncharacteristic surrender of control he wasn't sure he cared to repeat—except that it was probably part of the reason for the mind-blowing sex, which he *would* care to repeat.

He leaned over the sink and splashed water on his face, as if that might clear his senses. But when he straightened and took a deep breath he still smelled the flowers-and-sex perfume that was uniquely Lexie—this time with an odd, Italian-deli undertone from the olive oil. And when he looked at his reflection in the mirror, he saw the slightly redder patch of skin on his shoulder where she'd rested her head, and the sheen of oil on his chest like one of those bodybuilders in gym posters.

What exactly had happened back there? The question came again. He told himself it probably wasn't smart to overanalyze these situations. He'd had great sex with a beautiful woman who professed to not want any long-term commitment. Why not leave it at that and enjoy?

Except that his whole life revolved around analyzing situations, assessing risks, searching for clues and arriving at solutions. He couldn't shut that part of his brain off now.

And then there was the fact that Lexie wasn't just some good-time girl he'd picked up in a bar and brought home. She was his assistant and someone he was starting to think of as a friend, not to mention a woman who intrigued him as much as she turned him on.

All those things added up together worried him. It

meant there was a potential for things to get messy. She could say there would be no complications, just good times and then goodbye, but did those things ever happen outside of books and movies? This was real life here, and real life always got messy. As a cop he once knew was fond of saying, that's how you knew it was real.

A tap on the door interrupted his brooding. "Nick? You okay in there?"

"Yeah. Sure." He grabbed a towel and wrapped it around his waist, then immediately realized how stupid that was. He opened the door and she looked up at him. She was wearing one of his shirts, an old denim one with the sleeves rolled up past her wrists. She looked small and vulnerable and he fought the urge to sweep her into his arms and take her back to bed to make love until they were both too weak to stand.

"Um, I have to go to the bathroom," she said.

"Oh, sure. I'll just, uh, leave you alone." He moved past her and out the door.

"Nick?"

"Yeah?"

"Want to take a shower? We're both kind of, well, oily."

He glanced toward the shower stall, images of her soap-slicked body proving that his libido was revving up for round two. "Sure. I'll get some towels."

"And a fresh bar of soap. You're almost out."

He had vague memories of the sliver she'd used on him earlier. It had ended up somewhere on the floor by the bed. "Right." He hoped he had one. That was another thing about having a woman around on a regular basis. House-keeping mattered.

When he came back with the soap and towels, she'd

undressed again, though she was still wearing the scarf. She was combing out her hair in front of the mirror.

He hugged her from behind, his hands coming up to cup her breasts. He watched in the mirror as she set aside the brush and smiled at him. He couldn't believe he wanted her again so soon. It had never been like this with his wife, Monica, not even when they were first together. But Lexie was like some drug he'd become addicted to after one dose.

This was probably what celibacy did for you. That, and being with a woman who tied you up, greased you up and then made you forget your own name.

"Why don't you turn on the water?"

"Aren't you going to take off your scarf?"

She flushed, avoiding his eyes in the mirror. "I will in a minute. Turn on the water."

He opened the door to the shower stall and adjusted the taps. When steam began to fill the stall he stepped inside. She joined him seconds later.

He handed her the fresh bar of soap. "Ladies first."

But instead of using the soap on herself, she began lathering his body, using her hands and the soap bar on his chest and back. He held his arms up and let her wash his sides. "I could get used to this. Want to come over and give me a shower every morning?"

"Then we'd both be late for work." She began lathering his erection, her hands moving quickly back and forth, increasing his arousal.

He arched toward her, accidentally jostling her arm and sending the soap flying out of her hand. She squealed and they both bent to retrieve the bar, almost knocking heads.

She laughed. "Never mind. There's enough lather for

now." She shimmied against him, their skin sliding easily on the layer of soap.

"My turn," he said, and turned her so her back was to him. He scooped double handfuls of lather and covered her breasts, working her nipples between his fingers, enjoying the way she gasped and pressed her bottom against him. "Do you like that?"

"Yes."

"Your scarf's getting wet."

"I know." She hesitated, then reached up and untied it. "Promise not to look," she said.

He didn't answer. What could she possibly be hiding there that would take away from what he'd already seen?

But she kept her head turned away from him and slightly lowered.

It didn't matter. The water was cooling a bit, but still warm. He reached over and turned up the hot water, then he used his hands to spread lather down over her stomach and thighs to her clit. He slid two fingers into her, his erection stiff against her backside now.

She writhed beneath him, her hands braced on the shower wall. She was so gorgeous, so *into* it. He wanted to take her here. Now.

He moved his hands up to her breasts again, holding her tight against his chest. "Are you on any kind of birth control?"

She nodded. "The Pill."

"Any diseases? Have you been with anybody who might have given you something?"

"No. You're…you're the first since my accident. And I wasn't involved with anyone for a long time before that."

"Me, neither. Then it's all right if we don't use a condom?"

She nodded. "It's all right."

He started to turn her to face him, but she remained fixed. "No, let's do it like this."

She braced her hands against the tile again, bent slightly forward, legs spread.

He admired the view. She had a nice round ass, curvy and feminine, and gorgeous long legs. He grasped her hips and entered her from behind. She was tight and sensitive, using the wall for leverage to thrust back toward him.

With one hand he fondled her breasts, with the other her clit. He felt her tighten around him and braced his legs, grateful that the shower stall was small, the walls providing support for them both.

The water cascading around them and the remains of the soap added to the sensation of skin on skin. Their pace was more leisurely now, without the frantic quality of their earlier coupling, but just as intense.

He listened to her breathing change to mewling gasps and watched her fingers arched against the tile and knew when she was about to come. He increased his pace, driving deeper, his hand moving faster over her clit, satisfaction filling him as her cries echoed around them.

She bent farther forward, allowing him even deeper access. The added sensation drove him to his own climax.

Their cries gradually faded, replaced by the steady beat of the shower on the tile. He wrapped his arms around her and held her close, and kissed the back of her neck. Neither one of them said anything, just stood there, clinging together, as if reluctant to break the spell of contentment that was wrapped around them.

After a while he felt her shiver, and realized the water had grown cold. He slid out of her and, still holding her, turned her toward him and began to rinse the soap from her body.

She kept her head down, hiding her neck from him. He didn't press it. Whatever she didn't want him to see, it hardly mattered now.

When they were both free of soap, he shut off the water and helped her step out onto the bath mat. She took the towel he handed her and began to dry off, her back to him. He watched her as he used the other towel on himself, a little unnerved by the way she kept facing away from him, but there was nothing in her posture to indicate she was angry or upset. He decided this was her version of modesty. He handed her the denim shirt and she put it on, buttoning it high about her neck.

"Will you stay the night?" he asked.

"If you want me to."

"Yes." He doubted they'd have sex again, at least not for many hours. Right now he only wanted to sleep with her—really *sleep* with her. It had been a long time since he'd enjoyed that kind of companionship with a woman and he found himself looking forward to it.

7

LEXIE WAS DRESSING to leave when Nick awoke the next morning. "What time is it?" He rubbed his eyes and squinted at the clock.

"Five-thirty." She walked over to the bed and bent to kiss his forehead. "Good morning."

He yawned. "Do you always get up this early?"

"Only when I have to get back to my apartment and change so I won't be late to work."

"Yeah, I hear that boss of yours is a real bastard if you're late."

She laughed. "Actually, he only pretends to be fierce. But I know how to handle him."

"Maybe you'd like to demonstrate your technique again. Just to be sure I've got it down."

"Sorry, I really do have to go." She kissed him again, a quick peck on the cheek. "See you at the office."

She caught a glimpse of her reflection in her rearview mirror as she was driving to her apartment and realized she was wearing the most sublime grin. She probably hadn't stopped grinning since she'd gotten up.

And what woman wouldn't smile after the night she'd had? She felt as if every part of her body had been made love to and then she had slept as only a thoroughly satisfied woman could. She'd awakened with Nick's solid warmth beside her, and had indulged herself by watching him sleep. His hair was a mess, he snored and he needed a shave, but all that combined to make him seem so much more masculine and *real.*

She could be honest with herself now; writing down the goal of having affairs with six men before she was thirty had been an act of sheer bravado. After all, she'd never dated a great deal before. She'd been too reserved to take the initiative with men, and always felt as though she was probably missing out on a lot. She'd spent far more time hanging out with gal pals. So beginning even a short-term relationship with a man, which would mean spending a great deal of time together, had been a little daunting.

She credited her own intelligence and sheer good luck in finding Nick for her first attempt. Not only was he good-looking and sexy, he was also very understanding.

Take the whole thing with the scarves she wore. She knew he was curious about what she was hiding, but he didn't pressure her, or try to trick her into revealing her secret.

She slipped one finger under the edge of the scarf and glanced in the mirror again. The scrap of silk was definitely in sorry shape after its dousing in the shower. It probably looked worse than the scar she was hiding. She was being silly, really. Nick had seen everything else about her and obviously approved. One little scar wasn't going to send him running.

Still, the three-inch-long reddish-purplish gash at her throat looked horrible to her. And it was a reminder of how close she'd come to dying. She didn't like to look at it and she didn't like others looking at it, either. A scarf might invite curiosity, but people would ask questions about the scar. "What happened?" they'd ask.

She didn't want to talk about what happened. She didn't want to remember any of it. She wanted to focus on what was coming up in her life, instead. She had so many wonderful plans and dreams and making them all reality was the most fun she'd ever had. All the painful, lonely times were behind her. She wanted to create more joyful times like last night.

Was Nick grinning, too? She hoped so. He wasn't a man who smiled a lot, but if she had anything to say about it, he'd have many more reasons to smile in the next few months.

After all, she didn't want to be the only happy one. She wanted to share the good feelings and, right now at least, Nick was the one she wanted most to share them with.

NICK WASN'T SMILING as he talked on the phone with Stan Wittier. You'd think a guy would be happy to be told his wife wasn't cheating on him, but Wittier remained skeptical.

"On what do you base that assumption?" he asked.

"On the fact that I followed her for almost two weeks and never saw her with any other men. She never met anyone away from your home and no one came to your home while you were away."

"Perhaps she knew she was being watched."

"I don't think so. Besides, when I didn't turn up anything, I had my assistant approach her and strike up a conversation. They spent quite a bit of time together and my assistant assures me your wife is not being unfaithful."

"You sent your assistant to hit on my wife?" Wittier's

voice grew strident. "I believe that is completely uncalled for. And unprofessional."

Nick made a face. "My assistant is a woman. She met up with your wife in a nail salon and they went out to lunch. My assistant pretended to be a lonely wife considering cheating on her husband. Your wife was apparently appalled at the idea."

"That may be, but I believe I know my wife better than you or your assistant. She's clearly unhappy."

No joke. Nick was beginning to feel a lot of sympathy for Ellen Wittier. "I think your wife is unhappy because she's spending so much time alone when you're at work. While I was following her it was clear she spent far more hours every week by herself than she does with you."

"What are you accusing me of?"

"I'm not accusing you of anything. But I do think if you want to keep your wife faithful you might attempt to show her that she's at least as important to you as your business."

"I'm not paying you for marital advice."

"No, you're not. The advice is free."

"And worth less than that. I can see I've wasted my money with you."

"You'll be getting my bill." On that sour note, the conversation ended. Nick clicked off the phone and stared at it. What were the chances he was going to end up eating the costs of this investigation?

He shrugged off the worry and turned his attention to the other work on his desk, but background checks and skip-tracing couldn't hold his interest. He was still annoyed at Wittier's attitude. What if he'd been in Wittier's shoes? During those dark days right after his separation he'd have given anything for news that his wife wasn't cheating.

But unlike Wittier, he'd had no suspicions about Monica; she was the one who told him she'd found someone else. The knowledge that he'd been so clueless, so out of touch he hadn't seen it coming, still grated.

So was he wrong about Ellen Wittier, too? Was there something going on with her he just hadn't seen?

Too restless to sit behind a desk any longer, he abandoned his attempts at paperwork and went in search of Lexie. He could count on her to distract him from dark thoughts.

She had a stack of books on one end of her desk, though she was busy at the computer. "Are these for more classes?" he asked, picking up the top one and reading the title. *"The Simply Elegant Kitchen."*

"I'm taking a gourmet cooking class. And a lecture series on Spanish architecture."

"Don't you ever sleep?" He sat on the edge of her desk. Just listening to her list of activities made him tired. Not to mention he was beginning to wonder when she'd have time to see him again when she was so busy going to school in the evening.

"Of course I sleep." She laughed. "But not as much since the accident as I did before. Which is fine with me. Why waste time lying in bed when there's so much I want to do and see?"

He couldn't hold back a grin. "I don't consider all my time in bed wasted."

"Definitely not!" Her cheeks flushed pink but her eyes sparkled with amusement. Definitely an enticing conversation. He was about to ask when she'd be free to have dinner with him when the front door opened and a woman stepped in.

He stood and turned to greet the newcomer. She was an older woman, maybe mid-fifties, with graying brown hair cut short about her face and slightly stooped shoulders. "Hello. May I help you?" he asked.

She took two steps into the room and looked around her. "I hope so. I think I want to hire a private detective."

"I'm Nick Delaney and I'm a private investigator." He walked over to her and offered his hand.

She hesitated, then shook hands, her palms cold and dry. "Do you have experience finding missing persons?" she asked.

"Why don't you come into my office and we can discuss this more?" He put his hand on her shoulder and guided her toward his office.

"I'll make some fresh coffee," Lexie said.

He closed the office door behind them and ushered the woman to the chair across from his desk, then took his seat facing her. "How can I help you, Ms.—?"

"Trenton. Susan Trenton." Her gaze shifted around the room, taking in the innocuous framed paintings of ships at sea and the walnut wall clock that had all come with the space, and the bookcases full of policing manuals and texts relating to various crimes. Finally she looked at Nick again. "Do you know how to find missing persons?" she asked.

"Yes, I have some experience in that area. Who are you looking for?"

She dropped her gaze to her lap, and twisted the straps of her beige shoulder purse around the fingers of her right hand. "My brother, Oliver Bowman."

"How long has he been missing?"

"Three years. About that. The last time I saw him was

my birthday three years ago. He stopped by to give me a card." Her lips tightened and her nostrils flared as she sucked in a deep breath. "I never saw him again."

Nick fiddled with a pen on his desk, hiding his disappointment from the woman. Three years was a pretty cold trail. "Have you talked to the police about this? Do you suspect foul play?"

She shook her head. "I talked to them. But they said a grown man has a right to leave town and go away if he wants to. His landlady said he'd paid up the rent on his apartment through the end of the month, then packed his stuff into his car and drove away." She pressed her fisted hand against her mouth, her throat muscles contracting convulsively as she swallowed. "I can't believe he didn't even say goodbye," she whispered.

"Did the two of you argue about anything that last time you saw him?" The best way to handle this type of emotional situation with clients was to press forward, businesslike. It gave them time to compose themselves and stressed the impression that you were a professional.

Ms. Trenton sat up a little straighter and raised her head to look at him. "We didn't fight. I mean, sometimes I fussed at him for not taking care of himself. He's always been a bachelor and I know he doesn't eat right and he smokes too much. But we didn't fight about those things. He just let me rattle on and then went about things his own way, like always."

"Do you have any idea why he might have left so suddenly?"

She shook her head. "He was always restless, moving around a lot, but always before he'd let me know where he was. This time I haven't heard a word out of him in three years." She sighed, deflating against the chair. "It's not like we were ever terribly close, but all the rest of our family are gone now. We're the only ones left. It feels terrible not knowing where he is and if he's all right or not."

He took a standard contract form from his desk. "If you want to hire me to find your brother, I'll use all the resources at my disposal to do so, but I can't guarantee I'll find him." People who seriously didn't want to be found were almost impossible to locate unless they slipped up and broke the law or got careless about concealing their identity.

"I know." She took another deep breath and leaned toward him. "I've tried looking on my own, on the Internet, but I haven't found anything. I'm hoping a professional will have better luck."

He explained his fee schedule to her and went over the terms of the contract. "You can cancel at any time with a phone call or letter," he said. "And I'll provide itemized bills to show my time and what I've done to attempt to locate your brother."

She nodded and reached for a pen. "That's fine. I just want you to try. I want to know I've done everything I could." She raised her eyes to meet his; they were reddened and forlorn. "When you only have one person in your family left, it seems to me you ought to at least try to stay in touch."

"Yes, ma'am. I'll do what I can." He signed the contract and gave her a copy, then took out a legal pad. "I want you to give me as much information about your brother as you can. Age, height, weight, hair color, social security and driver's license numbers if you have them." He handed her the pad and a pen. "I'll need the address of every place he lived before and a list of jobs he's held—everything that might help us locate him."

"I'll try. Like I said, he was always restless. He had a lot of different jobs and lived a lot of places before he left."

"Take your time and try to remember as many as possible. And you can always contact me later if you remember something else."

There was a light tapping on the door and Lexie came in with a tray bearing two mugs of coffee, cream and sugar. She set the tray on the corner of the desk. "Can I get you anything else?"

He glanced at Ms. Trenton. "Maybe a box of tissue."

"I'm sorry." She covered her eyes with her hands. "It's just very upsetting."

"You don't have to apologize." Lexie retrieved a box of tissue from the supply closet and brought it to Ms. Trenton. "No one should ever apologize for their feelings." She touched the woman's shoulder. "Just remind yourself that you're doing something positive, hiring Nick. He's very good."

"He is?" Ms. Trenton uncovered her eyes, looking hopeful. "He is? Do you think he can find my brother."

She glanced at him. He frowned, hoping she'd get the message. Her faith in him was touching, but *don't make promises I may not be able to keep.*

She turned back to their client. "If anyone can find your brother, Nick can."

Ms. Trenton stared down at the legal pad in her lap. "Do you mind if I go home and write down the information you asked for there? I can't remember anything right now."

"That would be fine. You can bring the information by

anytime. And if you have any photographs of your brother, that would be helpful, too."

"I do have a photo." She brightened, and began rummaging in her purse. After a brief search she offered a small white envelope. "This was taken at Thanksgiving about five years ago."

Nick slid the snapshot out of the envelope. Lexie came around the desk and looked over his shoulder. The photo showed a slightly younger Susan Trenton and a thin, small-framed man with sparse brown hair and glasses. Oliver Bowman was a very ordinary looking man, the kind most people wouldn't look at twice on the street. The kind who could easily lose himself in a crowd. "This will be helpful," Nick lied, and replaced the photo in the envelope. "Now if you'd like to make your initial payment…"

"Oh yes, of course." She fumbled with her purse again, pulling out a checkbook and writing the check slowly. She studied it a few moments before handing it over. "I hope you can find him," she said.

"I hope so, too."

Lexie ushered Ms. Trenton out the door, then returned to his office. "Do you think you can find her brother?" she asked.

He shrugged. "Maybe. There are obvious things most people don't think of—driver's license records, property records. If he's drawing Social Security or disability pay I may be able to trace him that way. He may have been in contact with old friends his sister doesn't know about. But if he left town determined to disappear, it could be harder. If he changed his name and assumed a new identity, or if he went to another country, he may be more difficult to locate."

"Why would someone run away like that?" She looked

at the picture again. "Why leave and not tell anyone where you were going?"

"He could have been running away from something—a tax judgment, child support payments, a criminal record." He sank into his chair again. "I always have mixed feelings about cases like this."

She glanced at him. "Because they're so difficult?"

He shook his head. "No, I actually enjoy the challenge—digging into records, interviewing acquaintances, following up on leads. But invariably you find out things about the missing person the family would just as soon not know. Things that can tarnish the shiny image they've built up of their loved one."

"But that probably doesn't matter much if they're able to be reunited with the person they're trying to find."

"Maybe. But the fact that they *did* leave is always there, and not always easy to forgive. And then what if the person is dead?"

"Better to know for sure than to always wonder."

"I agree, but not everyone does. Some people get very angry. I've even had clients who refused to believe the person they've been searching for isn't there to be found."

She put her hand on his shoulder. "I guess I never thought much about the human side of this business—the personalities involved."

"In some ways, it's a lot more personal than police work. You tend to get more involved."

She looked at the picture again. "I wonder where he is. Why he left?"

"That's what I hope to find out. But if I find him, I have another dilemma."

"What's that?"

"What if he has a good reason for going away? A good reason for not wanting to be found? Or what if it isn't even a good reason, it's just what he wants? A man's entitled to live his life the way he wants to. He has a right to pack up and start fresh somewhere if he likes."

"Even if it hurts people who care about him?"

The tenderness in her voice worked its way past his carefully cultivated cynicism. "When you hired on, did I forget to give you the speech about not getting emotionally invested in our cases? About avoiding the danger of trying to 'fix' people's lives? We're hired to do a job and we do it. No judgment calls."

"I guess you forgot to give me that one. Besides, it's too late. I think detachment is overrated."

"You do?" This from the woman who had stressed she didn't plan on getting involved with him emotionally. As if sex and soul weren't tied together, however tenuously.

She nodded. "I think since every person is different, you have to treat every situation differently." The corners of her mouth turned up slightly. "After all, one-size-fits-all doesn't even work with clothes. It definitely doesn't work with people."

"You may be right." He gathered the picture and the signed contract and slid them into a file folder. "In any case, my job is to find Oliver Bowman, not figure out what to do with him. At least not yet."

"Right. Tomorrow you can show me how to search driver's license records." She moved toward the door. "Right now, I'd better go shut down the computer."

"Wait. You want to have dinner tonight?"

She stopped in the doorway. "It's tempting, but I have a class. Maybe some other time."

"Right. Some other time." He'd look forward to that, and not think about when there wouldn't be any other times. Unlike Ms. Trenton and her brother, he *knew* Lexie was going away one day. He even knew when. Would they stay in touch? Or lose track, the way he had with so many people he used to call friends? When he'd moved to Colorado he hadn't intentionally cut ties with the people he used to know, but he hadn't made an effort to contact them, either.

After all, a man had a right to start his life over if he wanted to. And Lexie had a right to leave her job and go to Spain and anywhere else. Two weeks ago, he'd been crystal clear on those truths.

But sitting here now, staring at the photo of Oliver Bowman, he wasn't so sure of his convictions. He'd focused all his thoughts before on the person leaving. Now he had to think about the person left behind. Things didn't feel so great from where he sat now.

8

NOW THAT LEXIE was helping Nick with the investigative side of his business, she looked forward to coming to work more than ever. She spent hours pouring over driver's license and social security records, searching for Oliver Bowman with no luck. While Nick talked to Bowman's former neighbors and employers, she did title searches in his name and called utility companies in various towns where he had connections.

"It's like trying to solve a puzzle with missing pieces," she told Nick as he guided her through the maze of a computer database one afternoon.

"It is something like that," he agreed.

"I get so excited when I find anything that might possibly help us." She scanned the list of names on the screen, hoping to find Bowman's. "Just think what a charge it would be to actually locate the man and reunite him with his sister."

"Even if we find him he won't necessarily want to talk to her."

Spoken like a true cynic. "At least we'll be able to tell Susan Trenton her brother is alive and safe—or dead and she no longer has to worry about him," she said. "And maybe finding out his sister has been looking for him will inspire him to get in touch with her again."

He shook his head. "You watch too many chick flicks. Real life doesn't usually work out that way."

"Some of us just aren't as cynical as you are." She glanced up at him. He was focused on the computer screen, jaw set in concentration, hair falling across his forehead. He looked strong and masculine and sexy as hell. It was all she could do not to reach up and brush the hair back, kiss his cheek. But right now he was her boss, not her lover, she reminded herself. It was important to keep the two separate.

As if aware of her watching him, his eyes met hers. "You say I'm cynical. I say I'm realistic. You can't expect happy endings in real life."

"I survived an accident that came close to killing me, so don't tell me about good things only happening in movies."

His gaze flickered to the scarf at her throat and he nodded. "One happy ending. I'll admit it happens some-times. But you can't count on it." He pointed to the computer screen. "Click here and let's try another section. Nothing's coming up yet."

She was scanning the new column of names when the front door opened and Stan Wittier entered, followed by his wife, Ellen. Heart in her throat, Lexie stared at the couple, who were focused on Nick and hadn't yet looked her way. The last thing she wanted was for Ellen Wittier to recognize her as the new "friend" she'd made at the nail salon. With no way to escape the room without being seen, she dove under the desk, sending her chair flying back.

"Hello there. How are you?" Nick's voice was overly hearty as he advanced across the room toward the Wittiers, perhaps an attempt to cover up Lexie's sudden departure.

"We wanted to talk to you, Delaney," Stan Wittier said.

"Then why don't we go into my office."

"Why?" Wittier's voice was abrupt, as usual. "I don't see anyone else here. Besides, this won't take long."

"Oh?" From her post under the desk, Lexie could only see feet—Wittier's brown wingtips, Nick's black boots and Ellen's high heels, a cunning confection of interwoven gold and pink leather accented with little leather flowers that Lexie immediately adored. Where *did* the woman shop for shoes?

"What Stan is trying to say is he's come to apologize." Ellen Wittier's voice was light and teasing, breaking some of the tension in the room. She was standing very close to her husband. Lexie imagined she was holding his arm.

Wittier cleared his throat. "I'm man enough to admit when I'm wrong," he said. "I've already apologized to Ellen for being wrong about her. Now I wanted to apologize to you. And to thank you for making me see the truth about my wife and our relationship."

"Stan's been a new man since you talked to him," Ellen said. "He's agreed to cut back some of his hours at work and this evening we're leaving on a second honeymoon." The happiness in Ellen's voice brought a lump to Lexie's throat. Maybe Ellen's lonely days and nights were over and she'd have the marriage she'd wanted all along. Now *that* would be a happy ending even Lexie hadn't anticipated.

"Thanks aren't necessary," Nick said. "I was only doing my job."

Lexie rolled her eyes. Such modesty. Stan Wittier would still be living at his office and wondering why his wife was so unhappy if Nick hadn't slapped him in the face with the truth.

"I also wanted to pay my bill." Wittier's shoes shifted as he apparently handed Nick a check. Lexie grinned. That would go a long way toward putting the office accounts back in the black.

"We'd better go, dear. We don't want to be late for our flight," Ellen said.

"Goodbye, Delaney. And thank you."

"Good luck to you both. Have a great time on your trip."

The door opened and closed again. Nick stood by the window a moment, then walked over to the desk. "You can come out now," he said.

She crawled out from under the desk and rose stiffly to her feet, brushing dust from her knees. "Speaking of happy endings…" She grinned at him.

"Yeah, I'm just a regular genie in a bottle, granting wishes left and right." He waved the check at her. "Wittier must have been in a really good mood when he wrote this. He included a little bonus."

"He can afford it." She peered over his shoulder at the check. "And you deserve it. You worked hard on that case."

"I seem to recall I had a little help." His eyes met hers, sending a definite heat through her. "We should go somewhere and celebrate."

She could think of a number of ways she'd like to celebrate with him. "We haven't finished the database search," she reminded him.

He glanced toward the computer. "We can finish tomorrow. Besides, it's already after five."

"It is?" How had she lost track of the time? "I have a class at six." She was sorely tempted to skip it, but she was barely keeping up with her Spanish lessons. Missing even one class might put her too far behind to ever catch up.

"Too bad." He didn't try to hide his disappointment.

"But maybe another night." She did a quick mental run through her schedule. "Tomorrow. I don't have class."

He folded the check and tucked it in his jacket. "It's a deal. We'll go someplace nice for dinner."

"How about my place?"

"Are you offering to cook?"

"I've been taking those gourmet cooking classes, remember. You can be my first guest."

"Mmmm. And do I get to stay for dessert?" He pulled her close and nuzzled her neck.

She wriggled out of his reach. Not because she wanted to be away from him, but because she knew if she stayed in his arms a second longer, she'd be *very* late for class. Besides, it never hurt to keep him wanting more. She collected her purse and books gave him a flirtatious look. "Play your cards right, and you could *be* dessert."

The spark of desire in his eyes this remark triggered was worth having to dodge out of his grasp on the way to the door. She hurried to her car, intent on getting to class, but wondering how much good it would do her. After all, she had a feeling she wasn't going to absorb much of tonight's lesson. Her mind would be too preoccupied with images of a certain handsome detective—with whipped cream and a cherry on top.

NICK SHOWED UP at Lexie's apartment complex on time, bringing with him a bottle of wine and a supermarket bouquet of flowers. He'd noticed she always had flowers on her desk at work. Every Monday he'd gotten into the habit of checking to see what this week's flower was. This Monday it had been yellow daisies, so he'd chosen a bunch of similar flowers, with some yellow and white carnations, for his gift tonight. He hoped she wasn't disappointed that they weren't roses. You never could tell with women. Monica always said he was clueless about what women wanted, but then, how were you supposed to know if they never told you?

So far, Lexie had been pretty good about telling him what she wanted. He smiled, remembering her visit to his apartment. Oh yeah, she'd left no doubt that night about *exactly* what she wanted from him.

He rang the bell at her door and looked around. It was a fairly modest neighborhood on the outskirts of downtown. A little worn at the edges but with the kind of rent she could manage on her salary. He promised himself he'd give her a raise as soon as he could afford to. She deserved it. She'd taken to the work, enthusiastic for even the dull stuff like database searches and filing. He appreciated her help, and he appreciated having her around to bounce ideas off of. Working alone for the past year, he'd forgotten how good it felt to talk over a case with someone he trusted.

Lexie opened the door. "Hi, Nick."

How was it dozens of people every day could address him by name and he never blinked, but when *she* said it his heart did a crazy dance step and he felt about two inches taller?

Then again, maybe it wasn't her voice that affected him as much as the sight of her in a white silk halter dress with a full skirt. And a white silk scarf tied at her throat. Talk about a gift-wrapped package....

"Won't you come in?" She held the door open wider and he walked past her into the living room.

"I brought you these." He handed her the wine and the flowers.

"How sweet!" She admired the wine, then buried her nose in the flowers, closing her eyes and inhaling deeply. Her cheeks glowed pink and when she looked at him again, her expression was full of light and energy. He wanted to capture that incandescent feeling and bottle it to take out on those days when life dragged at him.

"Come on into the kitchen and you can help me finish up our dinner." She led the way into a typical galley kitchen, every inch of counter space occupied by bags, boxes, pans, plates and two enormous cookbooks. "Just clear off a space and you can chop the salad ingredients," she said.

He took off his jacket and draped it over a bar stool, then moved aside one of the cookbooks and a stack of plates until he had a section of counter cleared to hold the cutting board she handed him. "What are you making?" he asked.

"Chicken fricassee. You can cut up some tomatoes, carrots, mushrooms and celery for a salad." She indicated a bag of produce that sat in the sink.

He selected a chef's knife from the rack by the stove and, after testing the blade against his thumb, reached for the sharpening steel. At the hiss of blade against steel, she turned around, startled. "What are you doing?"

"I like a sharp knife. Makes it easier to slice the vegetables and not my thumb."

He demonstrated, neatly dicing a stalk of celery in a few quick flicks of his wrist.

She laughed. "I'm impressed. And surprised. You didn't strike me as a man who knew his way around a kitchen."

"Hey, just because I was having frozen pizza the night you

came over doesn't mean I can't cook. But most of the time it doesn't seem worth it to go to that much trouble for myself."

"I know what you mean." She turned back to the pots on the stove. "One reason I took this class was because I thought it would help me get away from the whole frozen-dinner-for-one routine." She tasted the sauce, nodded to herself, then went back to stirring. "Did you cook when you were married?"

"Some." He raked sliced mushrooms into a bowl. He didn't want to talk about his marriage. He didn't even want to think about it when he was with Lexie. "Actually, my brother is a chef."

"No kidding? In Houston?"

"Yeah. He has a restaurant there, Cousins. Sort of country home cooking."

"How cool. Do you have any other brothers or sisters?"

"I have a sister who teaches junior high near Dallas." He selected a red pepper and sliced into it. "And then there's me, the black sheep."

"Why do you say that? Because you moved to Denver?"

He nodded. "I'm the only one who left Texas. The only one who got divorced. The only one who quit his job to strike out on his own." His parents still acted perplexed whenever he talked to them. He suspected they were waiting for him to come to his senses, move back home and put all the scattered pieces of his life together again.

"There's nothing wrong with being different," Lexie said. "Though it's hard when people you love have expectations that are so different from your own."

He crunched down on a bite of pepper. That was it, wasn't it? He usually didn't mind playing the rebel, but the thought that he wasn't living up to his family's expectations rankled. They didn't want the same things he wanted in life, the same way Monica and he had ended up with different goals. Was there ever going to be a time when he was in synch with those around him?

"What about your family?" he asked. "Do they live in Denver?"

"Durango. My mom works for Durango Mountain Resort and my dad has a job with the highway department. They love it. After the accident my mom came and lived here with me for a while, until I could handle things on my own. She talked a little about me moving back home but I think she recognized that wouldn't necessarily be a good thing."

"Because you'd depend on them too much?"

She laughed. "Because Durango's a small town. It's a great place, but there aren't a lot of jobs or stores or night-life or even that many single people my age." She lowered the burner under the big stock pot and replaced the lid. "Besides, after six months pretty much living in hospitals and stuck in this apartment, I'm more than ready to get out and see a little of the world."

Ah, yes. She was only here in Denver temporarily. In a few months time she was headed out of town, off to "go and do." Whereas he was just beginning to feel he might be able to settle down here, to sweep away the mistakes of the past and build something even better.

But he wasn't quite there yet. He supposed it was fitting that he and Lexie had gotten together while they were both in transition periods.

She collected the salad bowl from him. "Why don't you pour the wine and I'll bring dinner in in a minute."

He took the wine and the corkscrew she handed him to

the breakfast nook, which was occupied by a table set for two, and filled their glasses. In a moment she carried in a platter of golden brown chicken covered in a tomato-and-vegetable sauce. "I hope you're hungry," she said. "This recipe makes tons."

"It looks great." His mouth watered at the sight and smell of the food, but other appetites stirred as well as he watched her lean over to light the candles.

"Any new leads on Oliver Bowman?" she asked as she passed the salad.

He shook his head. "Record searches haven't turned up anything. None of his old employers have heard from him."

"So what do you do now?" She speared a piece of chicken and dropped it onto her plate.

"Next week I'll probably try to talk to some of his old neighbors, try to track down any friends. Though from what the employers told me he was kind of a loner. One of those guys who's off in his own world, doing his own thing."

"I guess investigating people, you get a unique perspective on what they're like."

"I get *a* perspective. I'm never sure if it's an accurate one." He sliced into the chicken breast. It was fragrant and succulent. "But most people, like Bowman's sister, only see one side of him. To her, he's her little brother who never could settle in one place or one job very long. To his neighbors or friends or people he worked with, he might be somebody else entirely."

"I guess we never really know people."

"Which is why people are so surprised when their son turns out to be a criminal or their spouse has another life

they know nothing about." Or how you can think someone's feelings and dreams are the same as yours and find
out you were way off base.

"What's the most interesting case you've ever had?" she
asked.

"The most interesting?" He considered this for a minute. "I was still with the police force at the time. There
were a series of thefts at the construction site of a multi-
million dollar home in River Oaks. Contractors were
losing tens of thousands of dollars in tools and building
materials. All the subcontractors checked out clean and
no one reported seeing anyone unusual around the site.
Finally we set up hidden cameras."

"Who was the thief?" she asked.

"Would you believe the owner of the house? The guy
had millions of dollars in assets and he's stealing from
some workmen trying to make a living." He shook his
head. "I'll never figure out some people."

"I guess law enforcement doesn't exactly expose you
to the nicest people in the world."

"There were good moments, too. I once helped recover
a ring that belonged to the wife of one of the Houston
Rockets basketball players. He was pretty grateful and
got me and my partner free tickets to a game."

"How did you recover the ring?"

"She suspected a workman who came to the house to
repair a window had nabbed it. We confronted him at his
apartment and he panicked and tried to get rid of the ring."

"Get rid of it?"

He laughed. "He swallowed it."

"What did you do?"

"We took him down to the station, locked him in a cell and waited for nature to take its course."

She laughed, rocking back and forth in her chair until she was breathless. "That's hilarious," she said on a gasp.

She dabbed the corner of her eyes with her napkin and sighed. "You've had such an interesting life. Mine has been so dull by comparison."

"Hey, don't knock it. Dull isn't so bad. It pays the bills and doesn't get you shot at."

She shook her head. "But you can still end up in a car wreck, or with cancer or in some other situation that can end it all like that." She snapped her fingers. "And then what have you got to show for it? When I woke up from my coma and realized how much time I'd wasted doing *nothing* I was appalled."

"So you made a list of things to do." He scraped the last of the chicken and sauce onto his fork. "How's that coming? Any more items checked off?"

"A few." She grinned. "It's a long list. And I keep thinking of things to add to it. That's what's so great about it. I always have something to look forward to."

He pushed aside his empty plate and drained his wineglass, then caught and held her gaze. "Right now I'm looking forward to dessert. How about you?"

"Definitely." She stood and collected their plates. "I made strawberry shortcake."

"That wasn't exactly the dessert I had in mind." He rose and came to stand behind her, pulling her close and nuzzling her neck. "I was thinking of something more…intimate. And even sweeter."

"Mmmm." She slipped from his grasp. "How about strawberry shortcake in the bedroom?"

"I think that could be arranged."

She looked over her shoulder at him, her gaze lancing through him, hot and melting as toasted marshmallows. "Then why don't you go on into the bedroom. I'll meet you there."

9

STEPPING INTO LEXIE'S bedroom was like walking into a jewelry box Nick's mother had had when he was child— all peach silk and femininity. The walls were painted a pale shade of blush and a quilted peach satin comforter floated atop the bed. Streamers of peach silk drifted down from a canopy above the bed and more of the same silk draped a dressing table. An oval mirror framed in gold hung above the dressing table. Framed nudes were arranged along the walls and unlit candles filled mirrored trays on the tables flanking the bed. Even unlit, he could smell the candles' scent: vanilla and spice, erotic and inviting.

Sliding doors across the room stood partway open, revealing Lexie's closet. He listened for her footsteps in the hall and, not hearing anything, crossed to the closet and nudged the doors open wider. He studied the neat rows of dresses, blouses and pants, remembering how she'd looked in each outfit. A dozen or more silk scarves hung from a circular tie rack. He brushed his hand through the fall of silk, letting it slip across his fingers. For someone who exuded so much self-confidence, here was her one sign of vulnerability. What was she so afraid of him seeing? Whatever she was covering up couldn't come close to all the ugliness he'd seen already in his life.

He heard footsteps in the hall and quickly moved out of the closet. She stood in the doorway with a tray. "Were you snooping?"

"Just curious. Let me help you with that." He rushed forward and took the tray, surveying the bowl or strawberries and can of whipped topping on it. "Where's the shortcake?"

"Hmmm." She feigned concern. "I guess I forgot it. We'll have to improvise."

"Did you forget plates, too? I don't see them."

She grinned. "Looks like I did. What will we do now?"

He set the tray on the dressing table and popped a strawberry into his mouth. The sweet juice exploded on his tongue when he bit down. "I guess we'll have to improvise."

He pulled her close and kissed her, the strawberry sweetness in his mouth mingling with her own subtle taste. He swept his tongue across her lips, exploring the soft sensuality of her mouth. She shaped her body to his, angling against him, her own tongue teasing him.

He deepened the kiss, the desire that had been simmering between them for days concentrated in that kiss, which left him dizzy and breathless and wanting more.

Lips still on his, eyes closed, she pulled his shirttail out of his pants and slid her hands up his bare back. Her fingers were cool, her nails scraping lightly, muscles contracting in her wake as she blazed a path up his spine.

He buried his face in her neck and worked his hand into the side of her top until he found her breast. She was firm and heavy in his palm, warm and smooth like sun-drenched fruit. His thumb found her nipple and strummed across the distended peak, eliciting a soft moan as she arched against him.

"I...if the whipped cream gets too warm it'll m-melt," she stammered, breathless.

"Maybe. Right now I'm going to make you melt." He pushed aside her top and bent to take the tip of her breast into his mouth.

She straddled his thigh, muscles squeezing, hands clutching his shoulders. "Wouldn't that be better...with a little whipped cream?"

"No. The only thing that would make it better is if you were naked." He pushed the dress off her other shoulder, then slid the bunched fabric down until it dropped off her hips and pooled at her ankles. Her underwear followed, and he steadied her while she stepped out of it. Now she was clad only in her scarf and white ankle-strap heels. She reached down to slip out of the shoes, but he clutched her wrist, stopping her. "Leave those on," he said.

Her eyes met his, dark and shining with unmistakable heat. He stepped back and began to undress, his eyes locked to her, wanting to see the effect he had on her. Her eyes followed his hands as he unbuttoned his shirt, slipped off his shoes and socks and unzipped his trousers. When he was naked, he motioned her over. "Come here."

She flowed into his arms, warm and pliant, her breath caressing his skin, her muscles firm beneath his exploring hands. He traced the indentation of her waist and the slope of her hip, lingering over her rounded bottom, noticing the almond paleness of her flesh against his sun-weathered hand.

She kissed his chest, her tongue painting a trail of moisture to his nipple, teeth scraping across that sensitive nub. He grunted and made a halfhearted effort to push her away, but she wrapped her arms around him and refused to budge. He felt the curve of her smile against his skin and she ground her pelvis against him as she began to suckle.

"Do you like this?" she asked, moving to his other nipple.

"What do you think?"

She slid her hand down between them and wrapped her fingers around his erection. "I think you do."

This was what she liked, wasn't it—calling all the shots, being in charge? Tonight it was her turn to be caught off guard a little. He took her by the wrists and held her, stepping away from her. "Not so fast," he said. "We've got all night."

She glanced toward the tray on the dressing table. "The whipped cream is going to melt."

He reached over and plucked a strawberry from the bowl and pushed it between her lips, his mouth following to taste the ripe fruit on her tongue. "Is this on your list?" he asked.

"Is what on my list?"

"Sex with food."

"Not exactly." She fed him a strawberry, the tips of her fingers slipping between his lips. He sucked hard, keeping her from leaving, his tongue playing across those sensitive digits, watching her pupils dilate and her expression tighten with desire.

When he released her, her hand dropped to rest on his chest, over his pounding heart. "What do you mean, 'not exactly'?" he prompted, reaching for another berry.

She blinked, and her eyes came back into focus. "I've decided to become a sensualist." She began massaging his chest, kneading the skin, following the light dusting of hair.

"A sensualist?" He tucked a lock of hair behind her ear

and suckled her earlobe. The fragrance of her perfume mixed with the scent of strawberries.

"Someone who pays attention to the five senses. How things taste and smell, feel and sound." She nudged his head up. "Close your eyes."

He hesitated, then decided to play along with the game. She was definitely…*creative* when it came to sex. And so far he'd benefitted greatly. Keeping his hands on her hips, he shut his eyes. "Now what?"

She fed him another berry, this time moving her fingers away before he could capture them. "Think about how it tastes," she whispered, her breath tickling his ear. "The sweetness. The tartness. The texture of the soft flesh on your tongue. The scrape of the seeds against the roof of your mouth. The sweet aroma. It smells like summer, doesn't it?"

Like summer. And like sex. He worked his tongue around the dissolving berry, aware of her hands around his penis again, her fingernails tugging at the sensitive skin stretched across his balls. He widened his stance, steadying himself.

"Your turn." He opened his eyes and looked at her. "Close your eyes," he prompted.

She closed them, her thick lashes a black fringe above her cheeks. He picked up the can of topping and sprayed three inches of whipped cream onto his finger. "Open wide."

Her mouth opened then closed around his finger, tugging at him, tongue wrapped around him, sending shock waves straight to his groin. "I think my cock's jealous," he said.

"Tell it I can't resist whipped cream," she said, sucking harder at his finger.

"Is that so?" He aimed the can toward his penis and depressed the button. The canned topping was cold and weightless, and began to melt as soon as it touched his hot skin. Lexie wasted no time sinking to her knees and wrapping her lips around him.

He groaned and gripped her shoulders as she worked to lick up all the cream. She was devastatingly thorough, bringing him to the edge of control.

As if sensing his growing tension, she took her lips from around him and stood, smiling. She had a smear of whipped cream on one side of her mouth. "Shall we get in bed?"

"We should." He kissed her, licking up the cream, then led her to the bed, where they lay down side by side. He got up almost immediately and retrieved the strawberries and cream from the tray. "We might as well finish these."

She grinned. "It would be a shame for them to go to waste."

He put a berry in his mouth and kissed her, both their tongues tasting the fruit. She reached for the can of topping, but he swatted her hand away and grabbed it himself. "Lie back," he instructed.

She did so, and watched, laughter dancing in her eyes as he dotted her breasts with the topping. He licked this up, his tongue flicking across her sensitive nipples long after every trace of cream was gone. "Nick!" she gasped, writhing beneath him.

He moved lower, and sprayed a curlicue of topping into her navel. When he began to lick it up, she giggled. "That tickles!"

"Does this tickle, too?" He laid a line of topping along her clit, then tossed the can aside to concentrate on cleaning up every last drop. He worked slowly, sweeping his tongue up and down that moist, sensitive pathway, suckling and teasing, aware of her increasingly desperate cries above him. He knew now that Lexie wasn't patient about waiting for anything.

"Nick, please," she gasped.

"Not yet." He wiped his mouth with the back of his hand and looked up at her. Their eyes met, hers pleading. "I don't want it to be over yet," he said. "I want to enjoy you longer." He slid up to lie at her side, one hand resting on her belly, maintaining the physical connection between them. "You said you wanted to be a sensualist. That means taking time to enjoy."

She gave him a half smile. "You're right. It's hard for me to slow down sometimes."

"It is hard." He wrapped her hand around his shaft, reminding her that he was aroused, too. Aching, but making himself wait, building anticipation. "Close your eyes," he whispered.

She closed them. He kissed each closed eyelid, then her temple, feeling the pulse throb against his lips. He trailed his tongue along her jaw, then to her neck, pausing to suck the soft flesh of her throat into his mouth, focusing on the smoothness of her skin against his tongue, the rasp of her breathing in his ear. She arched against him, the hard points of her breasts thrust up, inviting his attention. He smiled, excited by how much she wanted him. But he'd only just begun. He was going to see to it that she wanted him even more. Maybe more than she'd ever wanted any man.

LEXIE KEPT HER EYES CLOSED, trying to do as Nick had said, to focus on her senses. She listened for his breathing, but heard only her own ragged inhalations and exhalations. Was he really so calm, when she was all but frantic with need?

She put out her hand and buried her fingers in his hair, shaping her hand to the back of his head as he transferred his attention to her breast. As he drew one distended nipple into his mouth she let out a low moan. When he released her she moaned louder, bereft.

"Do you want me to stop?" he asked.

"No!" She wanted him to move faster, to hurry her toward what she knew would be an exquisite climax.

He chuckled. "Trust me. It will be worth the wait."

She admitted she was impatient. Waiting felt like wasting time, and she'd done too much of that.

Nick might see the logic in taking things slowly to build to a tremendous explosion, but as soon as one orgasm was over she could start the climb to another. So why waste time?

"Keep your eyes closed and tell me what this feels like."

Something brushed across her legs, light and cool, draping across her thigh, brushing against her clit. Something familiar… "Silk," she said. "The bed hangings."

"Very good." He pulled the swatch of silk away from her, dragging it across her sensitive center so that she gasped.

His mouth smothered the cry, even as his hand covered her mound, the heel of his palm firm against her clit, pressing down as she arched against him. His fingers and his tongue entered her at the same time, twin thrusts that occupied all her senses. The muscles of her vagina contracted around his fingers, and she moaned as he slid out of her again.

"Taste." He slipped his fingers between her lips and she

tasted the sweet/bitter flavor of her own juices. Is that what she tasted like to him? Did he like it?

As if to answer her question, he slid down her body and began kissing her thigh, working his way over to her clit. He covered her with his mouth, sucking gently, his tongue sliding back and forth across the sensitive nub. She arched against him, gasping. "Nick, please!"

He stilled, poised over her. "Please what?"

She raised her head and met his gaze. His eyes were dark, tight lines at the corners, his expression unreadable. "Please," she said again. "I can't wait any longer."

"Tell me what you want," he said.

"I want…I want you to make me come. Please."

"Since you asked so nicely…" He lowered his mouth to her again, his tongue stroking hard and fast, sending her spiraling out of control. She slammed her head back against the pillow and gripped at the sheets, dimly aware of a long, keening cry ripped from her throat.

Wave after wave of intense pleasure washed over her, overwhelming individual sensation in an onslaught of heat and light. As awareness returned, Nick knelt between her legs, the head of his penis poised at her entrance.

She arched toward him, anxious to feel him in her. He grasped her hips, holding back. "Still impatient, aren't you?" he asked, his eyes teasing.

"Aren't you?" She reached down and cupped his balls, squeezing gently, enjoying the sudden way his mouth went slack and his eyes glazed.

With a single thrust he entered her, filling her completely. He stilled, whether taunting her or gaining strength or merely savoring the intimacy of their joining, she couldn't tell. She smiled and smoothed her hands down his back, enjoying the feel of taut muscles and sweat-slicked skin.

He began moving again, rocking forward gently at first, then smoothly retreating. She met him thrust for thrust and the intensity and pace of each movement grew, until each thrust had him buried completely in her, and each withdrawal left only the head at her entrance.

The tension built within her again, spiraling quickly, as if her earlier climax hadn't been enough to satisfy the intense longing he'd created in her. She put her hands back, bracing against the headboard of the bed with each thrust, panting with both anticipation and exertion.

"Are you…almost there…again?" he asked.

She nodded, then afraid he might not notice, she spoke. "Yes."

He bent over her and took her nipple in his mouth, sucking hard. The effect was immediate, a second orgasm rocketing through her, stealing her breath.

He thrust harder still, the bed squeaking in protest. "Yes!" he shouted, and she felt the strong contractions of his own release. He continued to pump into her, gradually slowing, then relaxing completely, slumping onto her for a few seconds before rolling them both onto their sides.

He buried his face in her neck, breathing hard, the ends of her scarf fluttering every time he exhaled. For a long time neither of them moved, letting awareness steal back over them.

She closed her eyes and practiced being a sensualist. She noted the soft feathering of his hair beneath her cheek, and the scent of strawberries that still clung to him. She listened to the sigh of his breathing and thought she could make out the faint thump of his heart, in time with her own pulse. She felt the rough warmth of his palm as he cupped her breast, and the slight stickiness of her skin from the whipped topping. She felt him soften and slip out of her, leaving behind a more pronounced stickiness.

He draped his thigh over hers and pulled her closer. "Was that worth waiting for?" he asked, his lips close to her ear.

"Mmmmm. Maybe so."

"Maybe so?"

She smiled at the alarm in his voice, and laughed out loud when he raised his head to look at her.

"What do you mean, maybe?" he asked.

"I couldn't let you be right all the time, could I?" Still laughing, she cradled his head in both hands and pulled his lips down to hers.

"Even if you won't admit it, I know it was worth it." He spoke with his lips against hers.

"All right, I'll admit it. Sometimes patience *does* pay. But don't expect me to take things slow all the time."

"Next time, I promise, a quickie," he said. "Up against the wall. We won't even bother taking off our clothes." He nuzzled her neck.

She laughed. "I didn't say it had to be *that* quick."

"Yes, you did. I heard you. And I'm ready when you are." He slid farther under the covers and rested his head on her shoulder. "As long as you wait a few hours." He stifled a huge yawn. "Maybe tomorrow."

"So I get to decide, do I? That's nice to know. I'm a woman who likes to call the shots. I'll have to look at my list and see what else you can help me with. There are a few things on there I think might surprise you. I'm trying to explore my more unconventional side."

But she knew by his steady, slow breathing that he was already asleep. She smiled and kissed the top of his head. He could talk all he wanted to about taking things slowly but they wouldn't be here tonight if she hadn't rushed to act on her desire to have him as her lover. She wouldn't deny there was a time for a more leisurely pace, but not when it came to being with Nick. She wanted to enjoy every minute with him that she could before it was time to move on.

And she didn't want to think about when she'd have to leave him. It wasn't that she was anxious to be rid of him—far from it! But she had so many things she wanted to do with her life and who knew how long she had to do them? The only solution she saw was to keep moving forward. That would mean sometimes leaving people and places she cared about behind.

She closed her eyes, fighting the sudden sting of unshed tears. How had she let herself get on such a depressing train of thought? Nick obviously wasn't worried about the future. He'd agreed to an affair with her precisely because it *was* short-term. That was an ideal situation for him. So why should she worry about what would happen when their time together was up when he certainly didn't?

She took a deep breath and snuggled closer to him. The thing to do was to focus on the present. You couldn't change the past and you shouldn't worry about the future.

Trouble was, it was a lot more convincing when you weren't lying in a man's arms, feeling stronger and safer and more…*complete* than you ever had before. All the positive thinking in the world wasn't going to convince her brain that giving that up was ever going to be a good idea.

10

NICK HAD FACED DOWN armed robbers, been caught in the crossfire of gang wars, interceded in domestic violence incidents and endured the wrath of a woman whose boyfriend he'd just thrown in jail. But for the first time since his days as a rookie cop he felt as if he might have taken on a situation that was more than he could handle. Every day he was finding it tougher to pretend his relationship with Lexie was merely for fun and games. Every time he left her after they'd made love he felt the gnawing foreboding of trouble waiting to sneak up behind him.

Lust and loneliness had gotten the better of common sense from the very first when it came to Lexie. The minute he'd laid eyes on her long legs and looked into her quicksand eyes he'd known she had the power to hurt him. But he'd surrendered to her anyway. He could say it had been great so far, but she'd made it clear she didn't intend to stick around much longer.

And there wasn't a damn thing he could do about it. He was like a man tied to the railroad tracks, hearing the long moan of the train whistle and feeling the trestle shake, waiting for the end and wondering what it felt like to be cut in two.

This thought occurred to him as he waited for a freight

train to pass. He was headed to a bar over on Broadway, the Ten Spot. One of Oliver Bowman's old neighbors had told him this was a place where Oliver used to hang out. Nick was hoping someone there could give him a lead on the missing man.

The Ten Spot was sandwiched between a pizza parlor and a funeral home, a narrow deep saloon with a purple door opened to let in exhaust fumes from the traffic on Broadway and a steady stream of regulars. Nick stepped over the threshold and paused a moment to let his eyes adjust to the dim light. A black-and-purple bar ran the length of the room on the left while tables and chairs crowded the space to the right. A neon-trimmed jukebox squatted in the back corner, pumping out vintage Johnny Cash tunes.

He took a seat at the bar and ordered a draft beer. The bartender was a young guy, with an Elvis pompadour and tattoos running the length of both arms. He was probably too young to have known Oliver, but Nick would ask anyway. One thing he'd learned a long time ago was not to make assumptions.

"I'm looking for a guy who used to hang out here," he said when the bartender returned with his beer. "An older guy, named Oliver Bowman. You know him?"

The young guy shook his head. "I've only worked here about nine months. You might ask Darlene. She's been here forever." He nodded toward a spike-haired blonde who was chatting up a customer at one of the tables. In her low-slung jeans and pink tank top, she didn't look much older than the bartender from behind, but when she turned toward the bar Nick saw that she was probably closer to forty than twenty.

"Hey, Darlene," the bartender called. "This dude says he's looking for somebody named Oliver who used to hang out here. You know him?"

The waitress said something to her customer, then came over to Nick. "You mean Ollie Bowman?"

"That's him. You know him?"

"Yeah. He used to come in here." She stashed her tray behind the bar and rested her elbows on the scuffed countertop. "He was a sweet guy. Haven't seen him in a while, though. A few years."

This was the first time he'd heard Oliver referred to as sweet. Most people said he was quiet or a loner, even odd. "How well did you know him?"

She shrugged. "Pretty well, I guess. He was in here almost every day. Sometimes he'd get a pizza from next door and we'd split it."

"What was he like?"

"He was smart. He knew about a lot of stuff like politics and the environment and music. He cared about stuff." She shook her head. "Maybe too much."

He took a long sip of beer, digesting this information. "What do you mean?"

She shook a cigarette from a pack on the shelf behind her, then lit it with a lighter from her pocket. She inhaled deeply, exhaling twin plumes of smoke from her nose. "It really upset him when people didn't care about things the way he did. He used to argue a lot about that."

"Who did he argue with?"

"Other customers. His sister." She took another long drag of the cigarette.

His left eye twitched, a sure sign that he'd alerted on something important. Oliver's sister certainly hadn't mentioned anything about arguments with her brother. "He and his sister didn't get along?"

She tilted her head to one side, considering the question. "I wouldn't say that. I mean, Oliver wasn't really close to anyone. That wasn't his way." Her eyes narrowed. "Hey, why are you asking so many questions? You a cop?"

He shook his head. "I used to be. Now I'm a private detective. A friend of Oliver's is looking for him." Better not mention the sister. "Have you heard from him lately?"

She tapped ash into a chipped glass. "Not in years."

"How many years?"

She frowned. "Three? Four? He came in here one day said he was going away for a while."

He drained his beer mug, suppressing a flutter of excitement. "Did he say where?"

"No. I didn't ask. He was a private person." She stubbed out the cigarette. "People who knew him respected that. We didn't pry."

"Where do you think he might have gone?"

"The mountains." She shrugged. "Or the desert. Somewhere people would leave him alone. We used to tease him, say he'd make a good hermit."

"What kind of hermit hangs out every afternoon at a place like this?"

She shrugged. "You had to know Ollie to understand. Seemed like he wanted to be *around* people, but he was never really *with* them. It was more like he was, I don't know, *studying* them or something."

Bowman wanted company but didn't want to be involved. Nick could sympathize, though he'd never been able to keep from involving himself in others' lives. It was one of the hazards of his work, and one of the reasons he'd developed an attitude Lexie thought was cynical. Was Bowman a cynic, too? Is that why he held himself apart from others?

"He never mentioned anywhere specific he might go?" She shook her head. "I don't remember anything. Sorry."

"That's okay. Thanks."

She picked up his empty mug. "You want another beer?"

"Sure."

She served him the beer, then went over to the jukebox and fed in quarters. Dolly Parton began to sing about Jolene taking her man. Three workmen came in, in dirty jeans and steel-toed boots. Darlene greeted them by name and they ordered beers and shots. The Railbenders sang about O-D-ing in Denver and Nick finished his beer, enjoying the beginning of a buzz. Maybe he'd call up Lexie, see if he could drop by. Maybe buy her dinner. Take her up on her offer of a quickie.

Darlene stopped by to collect his empty beer mug and he declined her offer of another. "I just remembered something about Oliver," she said as she wiped the counter in front of him.

He sat up straighter, alert, waiting.

"He used to talk about going to Glenwood Springs sometimes. He thought it was a real spiritual place, with the springs and all. He used to say he wished he'd gone there to live instead of settling in Denver."

"Thanks. I'll check it out." He left a twenty for the beers and her tip and left, walking slowly to the lot where he'd parked his car. It wasn't much, but it was a start. Maybe Oliver Bowman wasn't anywhere near Glenwood

Springs but there was at least a chance he was. Nick would do a quick computer search for the area but if that didn't turn up anything, he'd plan a trip there to check things out.

Maybe he'd even ask Lexie to come with him. After all, she was his assistant as well as his lover. And to think he'd once thought that would be a bad combination.

"I'D LOVE TO GO to Glenwood Springs with you." Lexie somehow refrained from doing a gleeful dance in her chair when Nick issued his invitation. Seeing Nick one or two nights a week whenever they could get free was fun, but several days—and nights—in each other's company held all kinds of tantalizing possibilities.

"Have you been there before?" he asked.

"It's been a few years." More than a few, really. She'd gone with her family when she was a girl, but somehow she'd never made it out there since she'd been out on her own. All the more reason to visit it now. "It's one of my favorite places in Colorado." She had fond memories of soaking in the legendary hot springs and walking along the river that wound through Glenwood Canyon.

"Good. Research goes a lot faster when you have someone with you who knows where things are, how the city's laid out and all that."

"So this is a research trip?" She tried not to let her disappointment show. And here she'd thought Nick was interested in a little vacation with her.

He propped one hip on the corner of her desk. "A waitress at a bar where Oliver Bowman used to hang out says he talked a lot about going to Glenwood Springs. It's a long shot, but we might as well check it out."

She picked up a pencil and idly tapped it against the

side of her computer monitor. "If someone really wanted to hide, why not go farther away? Another state, even?"

"Maybe we'll find out the answer in Glenwood Springs."

"Maybe." She dropped the pencil back in the coffee cup that doubled as a pen holder. "If nothing else, it'll be a nice break from the office."

"You understand we'll be working. I'll probably want you to do some checking at the courthouse while I talk to people around town." Nick tried for a serious expression, but the light in his eyes gave him away. She played along.

"Oh, absolutely." She banished her smile and assumed a this-is-serious-business frown. "I wouldn't dream of even thinking about anything but work while we're away." She sat up straight and folded her hands primly in her lap. "I promise to leave my bathing suit and my new *Victoria's Secret* lingerie at home."

He shifted his position on the edge of the desk. "Now, I don't want you to think I'm the kind of boss who'd expect you to work all the time. I'm sure we'll both deserve to relax a little in the evenings after working hard all day."

"Does this mean I should pack my bathing suit?" She looked up at the ceiling, lips pursed in a thoughtful pout. "After all, it would be a shame to go to Glenwood Springs and not take advantage of the hot springs."

He cleared his throat. "Pack the suit. And the lingerie."

She laughed and he joined her. "There's no law that says we can't work and enjoy ourselves, right?" she said.

"Right." He stood. "Will you call a hotel and make reservations for a couple of nights?"

"All right." She clicked on her computer, prepared to

sign on and research Glenwood Springs motels. Nick collected the day's mail from her in-box and headed for his office. A train whistle sounded over the rumble of traffic on the street and she sat up straighter, struck with a brilliant idea.

"You know, if we're going to go to Glenwood Springs, we really ought to take the train," she said.

He stopped in the doorway of his office. "The train?"

"Sure." She swivelled her chair toward him. "Amtrak leaves from Union Station headed west every morning. It's spectacular scenery, through Winter Park and the Moffet Tunnel and Glenwood Canyon."

Frown lines made twin furrows across his forehead. "I don't know. I wasn't planning on taking that much time."

"We can be there after lunch." She threw in her trump card. "Besides, it's on my list."

"What's on your list?"

"Number forty-seven. Making love on a train."

Their eyes met, heat arcing between them like sparks across uninsulated electric lines. "Then I guess you'd better call Amtrak."

"I'd be happy to." She turned and reached for the phone, managing to suppress her grin until he'd entered his office and closed the door. Thanks to Nick, she was getting quite a few items on her list checked off. What then? When the list was done, would she be ready to relax and settle down? Settling down was the last thing she'd wanted when she'd gotten out of the hospital but now…? Well, staying in one place for a while might not be so bad. Not if you found the right person—the right man—to stay with.

She shook her head. *Don't even go there,* she told herself. She and Nick had made a deal. They were together to have a little fun. No commitments. It was what they both wanted.

Or at least, what she'd thought she wanted. Now she wasn't so sure.

"I'M SO GLAD you were free tonight," Lexie said as Candace pulled her Jetta into a parking space at Cherry Creek Mall. "No woman should have to buy a swimsuit without another woman along to give her an honest opinion."

"As if you'd look bad in anything." Candace switched off the car and checked her lipstick in the visor mirror. "But you know me—I'm always up for hunting and gathering at the malls. Not to mention I haven't seen you in ages."

"Only a couple of weeks." Lexie felt a twinge of guilt as she climbed out of the car. "I know it sucks, but I've been so busy."

"I know. And because you're my best friend, I forgive you." Candace stowed her sunglasses in her purse and led the way to the elevators.

"So where should we look first?" Lexie asked as they waited for the elevator to arrive. "Tommy Bahama's? PacSun?"

"I saw BeBe is having a sale on summer clothing. That probably includes swimsuits."

"I hope so. I want something stellar for next week."

Candace grinned. "So tell me more about this trip. Why is Nick taking you to Glenwood Springs? Does this mean things are getting serious between you two?"

"Of course not." Lexie stumbled getting on the elevator, but caught herself and turned to stare at her friend. "Why would you think that?"

Candace shrugged. "You've been spending a lot of time with him, haven't you? And now you're going on vacation together. Sounds like things are heating up to me."

"Things are pretty hot, all right. But not in the way you're talking about. I mean, they can't be."

The elevator opened, discharging them across from the Cherry Creek theater. "BeBe is down this way," Lexie said, turning left.

"What do you mean they can't be?" Candace asked.

"Nick and I didn't get involved to be serious," she said. "Neither one of us is at a place in life where we're ready to settle down."

"So going away on vacation together is just more fun?" Candace looked skeptical.

"Of course. Besides, this trip isn't really a vacation. We're going to be working." She halted in front of a window display of swimwear at Tommy Bahamas. "What do you think of that red bikini? The one with the metal stud trim?"

Candace raised one eyebrow at the tiny, wet-look vinyl suit. "I think you won't get much work done if you wear something like that."

She laughed and led the way into the store. "We won't be working all the time. We'll have some fun, too."

"So that's all that's between you two—work and fun?"

"What more could I want?" She rifled through a rack of swimwear, searching for the suit that would flatter her the most while wowing Nick.

"I don't know." Candace pulled out a purple tankini, frowned at it, then shoved it back on the rack. "Love? An engagement ring? Aren't those things most women our age are interested in?"

Lexie ignored the way her breath caught at the image that flashed through her mind of Nick presenting her with a large diamond ring. "I'm not interested in those things," she protested. "At least, not right now. I have too many other things I want to do first."

"Right. Your list. How could I forget?" Candace rolled her eyes.

"Don't look at me like that! You thought the list was a great idea when I told you about it."

"It is, but…"

"But what?"

"But I worry you're trying to do too much. You never slow down anymore."

Who wanted to slow down? Living slow left too much time for thinking. For second-guessing your decisions, or regretting past mistakes. Better to think less and live more. Slow was boring. "It only seems that way to you because you don't see me every day anymore." She selected two suits off the rack. "Trust me, I'm not doing too much. I get to bed early almost every night."

Candace laughed. "Going to bed with your hot lover doesn't count as rest."

"I didn't mean those nights." Lexie laughed, too. God, she'd missed hanging out with Candace this way.

Candace worked her way around the rack toward Lexie. When she was standing beside her she leaned toward her and spoke in a low voice. "So…how many items on your list have you and Nick managed to cross off together?"

"A few."

"You're blushing." Candace shook her head. "Though I'll admit, some of those things would have made me blush, too."

"Don't knock it 'til you've tried it." Lexie felt her cheeks grow warmer. "You might enjoy yourself." Lexie had certainly had an amazing time "experimenting" with

Nick. Of course, he deserved much of the credit. No matter what wild idea she proposed, he went along with it—and made the moment special.

"If I had a guy like Nick around, I just might do that." Candace selected a black lace bikini from the rack and held it out. "What do you think of this?"

"Oooh. I *like!*" She took the garment from Candace. "I'll try it on." She returned to her search of the racks, considering, then discarding a snakeskin one-piece. A tank suit was great if you intended to do any serious swimming but for her purposes she required a suit that would make Nick's eyes pop. That required one that showed as much flesh as legally possible.

She selected a halter-top suit in a pink abstract print. "You should try this one," she said, offering it to Candace. "It's in your size."

"It's cute." She took the suit. "I guess I could keep it on hand in case a guy ever asks me to go on vacation with him. Though the way my luck's running by the time that happens it will be out of style."

"What about that new hot guy at work? The one who took my place?"

"As if! He doesn't know I exist, believe me. Not with every female in the building hitting on him." Her voice rose to a saccharine falsetto. "'Charles, can you help me with this project? Charles, can you fix the copier? Charles, why don't we have lunch? Charles, want to meet for drinks?'"

Lexie laughed. "What does Charles do?"

"Oh, he flashes that gorgeous smile and fixes the copier or helps with the project or goes out for lunch or drinks. And apparently never does anything more. Or else he's incredibly discreet, which I'm not buying. There's no such thing as real privacy in a small department."

"You're right about that." Lexie added a fourth suit—an orange retro style—to her growing pile. "You said he was straight, right?"

"Yeah, I'm pretty sure of that. Roberto in the mail room says he is."

"Roberto would know. Okay, so maybe he's immune to flirting and innuendo. Maybe you need to take a more direct approach."

"Me? What are you talking about?"

"Ask him out. Proposition him if you're bold enough."

"Right. This from the woman who lusted after Mike Consuelo in accounting for six months—until Tanya Sebold stole him right out from under your nose."

Lexie winced. Last she'd heard, Tanya and Mike were happily married. Not that she still felt anything for Mike, but she'd always have to wonder, *what if?* "So you can learn from my mistakes," she said.

Candace shook her head. "I couldn't do it. I would never have the guts."

"Sure you do. Whatever you really want is worth going after." No telling where she'd be today if she'd taken more chances earlier in her life.

"I don't know if I really want Charles. I mean, he's good-looking and funny and smart and has a good job and is pretty much perfect, but other than that, why would I want him?"

Their eyes met and they both doubled over laughing. "Yeah, I see your point," Lexie said between giggles. "What woman would want a man like that?"

"Besides," Candace said. "We all know a guy may look

perfect from a distance, but as soon as you get to know him, all his bad habits and character flaws come out of hiding. Maybe you have the right idea after all."

"What idea is that?"

"Have an affair with a great guy, then when things turn out not so great move on. No guilt involved. No strings attached." She nodded. "It's probably a very healthy attitude to have. More mature than the happily-ever-after fantasy the rest of us are holding on to."

"I don't know about that." Lexie shook her head. After all, she hadn't entirely abandoned that "happily-ever-after fantasy." She'd merely put it on hold while she got a little more living under her belt. "I'm going to try on these suits," she said, turning toward the dressing rooms.

"Me, too. At least then if Charles ever notices me I'll be ready."

"That's great. You should always be ready for good things to happen." But Candace's earlier words still nagged at her. Had she been spending so much time getting ready for the next good thing that she hadn't focused enough on enjoying what she already had?

11

"I'VE NEVER BEEN ON A TRAIN," Nick confessed as he and Lexie boarded the westbound California Zephyr at Denver's Union Station the next Wednesday morning.

"Then you're in for a treat," Lexie said as she led the way to a pair of seats near the back of the car. "You see things from the train that you'll never see in a car."

"I can't wait." He smiled to himself as he followed the enticing sway of the chiffon skirt that flowed over her shapely bottom. He had no doubt some of the most interesting scenery would be inside the car.

"Glenwood Canyon alone is worth the price of a ticket." She stowed her backpack in the overhead bin, then slid into the window seat. "But it's not just the scenery that makes train travel so great. I love it because it's so relaxing. You really get a chance to slow down and enjoy things."

"What sort of things?" He sank into the seat next to her and stretched out his legs.

"Oh, all sorts of things." She winked, a surprising gesture that sent an odd tremor through his chest. He'd never met a woman with a knack for keeping him off-balance the way Lexie did. Take this train trip, for instance. She'd lured him here with a sexual come-on but he'd found himself looking forward to the chance to spend a few hours in her company, out of bed and uninterrupted by telephones or other people or any kind of schedule.

The train whistle let out a long blast and the cars started forward with a jolt. Union Station's ornate facade receded as the Coors Field scoreboard loomed over the tracks. "Have you ever been there?" Lexie nodded toward the ballpark.

He shook his head. "I haven't made it there yet."

"You should. It's a gorgeous place. And you should take in a Broncos game sometime, too. Denver's a great town for sports."

"I didn't know you were such a sports fan." He rested his arm across the back of the seat they shared, letting his fingers trail onto her shoulder.

"I like some better than others." She quirked one eyebrow in a flagrantly sexy come-on.

"Such as?"

"Maybe I'll give you a demonstration later. If you behave yourself."

"And let you have all the fun? I don't think so."

She turned back to the window, but not before he saw the knowing smile that tipped up the corners of her mouth. A familiar tension coiled in his groin in anticipation of what he might be in store for later.

The train steamed through the back streets of Arvada then entered open country and began climbing the foot-hills northwest of Boulder. The imposing red granite slabs of the Flatirons thrust up against a turquoise sky while Boulder Creek wound through the valley like a strand of tinsel caught in the trunks of the thick stands of pine.

"It looks like a postcard," he said.

"You should go hiking around here," she said. "There are some incredible views from up top."

"I haven't worked that into my schedule, either."

She glanced over her shoulder at him, her expression stern. "Living in Colorado, you need to take advantage of these things. Just think—people spend all kinds of money to come here on vacation and you've got it all here in your backyard."

"Guess I've been too busy getting settled." He shrugged. "I'll have to add it to my list."

She brightened. "Are you going to start a list of things you hope to accomplish, like mine?"

"I don't think so." He leaned closer, slipping his arms around her. "I think I'd rather help you with your list. Did you say there's something on there about a train?"

"Maybe." She snuggled closer. "Don't you think the rhythm of the cars rocking on the tracks has certain possibilities?"

"I see what you mean." He slid his hand up to cup the underside of her breast. Holding her like this was like holding sunlight—all heat and energy and pulsing life. He could feel her heartbeat, strong and steady beneath his thumb.

He closed his eyes and counted beats—one, two, three—and breathed in the scent of her hair, sweet and floral. He'd always considered himself a practical person, but being with her had him daydreaming about stopping time. He wanted to memorize the softness of her skin, the slide of her silk blouse against his chest, the way a flyaway strand of her hair tickled his chin.

"Mmmm. This is nice." She slid her hand up his thigh.

And getting nicer by the minute. He moved his hand higher, covering her breast now, pretending to focus his gaze on the scenery rolling by outside the window while he felt her nipple harden against his palm.

She reached back and flipped up the armrest between them, then turned toward the window again and snuggled her back more firmly against him. "I like that," she murmured.

He unfastened the top button of her blouse and slid his hand beneath the fabric, easing into her bra until he caressed her bare breast. Facing the window this way, with the high seat-backs shielding them from view in the almost-empty car, he was fairly certain no one would see them. He kissed her neck, his tongue flicking across the soft skin, tasting salt. "What else do you like?" he asked.

She continued to gaze out the window, her hand stroking lightly up and down his thigh. "What do I like?" Her fingers shaped to his leg, squeezing gently. "Lately, I like taking risks. Doing things that are a little bit…dangerous."

The answer surprised him. She hadn't struck him as the daredevil type. A little adventurous, maybe, but not into danger. "What kinds of things?"

"Oh, I don't know. Maybe walking a little close to the edge when I'm hiking in the mountains. Or taking curves a little too fast when I'm out driving. I'd like to go sky-diving one day, too. I haven't done that yet."

"Hmmmm." He unfastened two more buttons on her blouse and laid his hand across her belly. He traced the indentation of her navel, and remembered kissing her there. "Have you always been a risk-taker?"

"Only since my accident." She slid her hand up to cover the hard ridge of his erection at his fly. "Before that I was very conventional. Timid, really."

He sucked in a sharp breath as she squeezed him, fighting the urge to grind against her. He tried to picture her as timid, but under the circumstances that was impossible. "Why did you change?"

"I spent so much time in the hospital, all my senses muffled by drugs and pain and sterilized surroundings. When I finally got out I *craved* sensation. I wanted to feel everything as intensely as possible. And I discovered fear or anxiety has a way of focusing all your senses acutely." She traced one finger the length of his fly, laying a trail of sparks that had him biting his lip, stifling a groan.

He slid his hand out of her shirt and locked his fingers around her wrist, stilling her. "Is that what led you to apply for the job at my office? Because you thought it might be dangerous?"

"I thought it would be interesting." She swivelled to face him. "And I thought *you* would be *very* interesting."

"May I have your boarding passes, please?" A conductor in a blue jacket and cap loomed over their seats, a bored expression on his mustached face. He collected the boarding passes without comment and checked them against his passenger list. "You're going to Glenwood Springs?" he asked.

"Yes. My friend here has never been," Lexie said, her face flushed, eyes bright with excitement. Did the conductor notice that her shirt was unbuttoned to her waist, or that Nick had a definite hard-on? "He's never been on a train before, either."

"Hmmph. I've been on too many." Without another glance in their direction, he left them and exited the car.

Nick leaned toward Lexie. "Good thing he didn't come by a few minutes earlier."

"I don't know. If he had, maybe he wouldn't think of his job as so dull anymore." She rested her hand on his knee, her eyes alight with mischief. "That's half the fun, isn't it?" she said. "The chance that you might get caught?"

"There's the idea of risk again."

She reached up and began to unbutton his shirt. "It adds a certain…excitement, doesn't it? An…edge." She finished unbuttoning and tugged the shirttail out of his jeans, then slid her hands up his torso to his chest.

"I suppose it does." He angled his body more sharply toward her, grateful no one was seated near them.

She leaned toward him and kissed his neck, her fingers playing across his nipples. "Your need is so urgent, you want to go fast, but you know you have to take it slow." She moved her mouth lower, feathering kisses along his collarbone, while her shirt fell open to reveal the tops of her breasts swelling over the lace of her bra.

"Maybe we should stop." He closed his eyes and nuzzled her hair, not meaning the words.

"Oh, no, we can't stop." She slid her hands around to his back, under his belt to brush the top of his buttocks. "Not when it feels so good."

"What if the conductor comes back?" he asked, feeling an extra jolt of arousal at the thought.

"We'll have to be very quiet," she said, her voice low and throaty. Seductive. She raised her head and, eyes locked to his, she unfastened the front catch of her bra, freeing her breasts. "We can't moan, or cry out, or make a sound." She leaned into him, pressing her chest to his, her nipples hard points between them.

Even if the conductor had walked up and stood over them, Nick didn't know if he would have paid attention. She had him fully aroused though they were both still mostly dressed.

She reached for the zipper of his jeans and he put his hand over hers, buying time while he caught his breath and tried to think. "What do you think you're doing?" he asked.

Her eyes met his, her gaze hot, raising his own temperature another notch. "I'm going to make love to you," she said. "You're going to be breathless and hot and half out of your mind with wanting me."

He was most of the way there already. "It's broad daylight," he said, fighting to maintain a sense of reason in spite of the throbbing between his thighs and the sight of her breasts swaying slightly in the shadowed opening of her shirt. "It's not even ten o'clock in the morning. We can't just go at it like two dogs, where anyone could see."

"Of course not." She took his hand placed it on her knee, then guided it up her thigh, up under her skirt. "We'll wait for the tunnel."

He laughed nervously, even as his brain registered that she was very naked underneath her skirt. "I don't think a tunnel will be long enough."

"Oh, but you haven't seen this tunnel. It's lo-o-o-ong."

"Yeah?" He slipped his hand between her thighs. It was warm and moist there; the thought that she was as ready as he was added to his anticipation. "How long?"

"Over six miles."

He blinked. "You're kidding."

She laughed. "No, I'm serious. It's a tunnel under the Continental Divide." She unfastened the top button of his jeans. "We'll be in the dark for almost fifteen minutes."

"I see you've done your research."

"I said I like to flirt with danger—that doesn't mean I don't believe in being prepared."

He eased two fingers into her, his heart racing as she tightened around him. "So when do we get to this tunnel?"

"Soon." She leaned forward and kissed him, her tongue probing his mouth as she lowered his zipper. "Very soon."

LEXIE WAITED, motionless, her hand on Nick's zipper, their mouths together, eyes closed. She waited, anticipation building with each turn of train wheels against metal track. She could feel Nick's fingers in her, arousing her further even in their stillness. Every second they remained like this made her want him more. It was all she could do not to cry out in frustration at having to wait, but she'd planned this very carefully. The timing had to be right….

Their car plunged into darkness as they entered the tunnel and she arched forward, driving Nick's fingers deeper into her. The sensation was incredible, as if she was balanced on his hand in the darkness.

Of course, as her eyes adjusted she could see it was not so dark. A security light glowed at the far end of the car and close to that an older woman had turned on her overhead reading light. But their end of the car was still shrouded in shadows, private and mysterious.

"We'd better hurry," Nick urged, withdrawing his fingers and pushing aside her blouse and open bra to allow him access to her breasts. She gasped as he sucked one nipple into his mouth, and felt a fresh jolt of heat and moisture between her thighs.

She clutched at his head, pulling his back. "It's okay. We have plenty of time."

He acted as if he hadn't heard her. His mouth contin-ued to torture and tease, his teeth lightly raking her sensitive nipples, then his tongue sweeping over them to soothe. She arched to him, giving herself up to building desire.

The thunder of the train on the tracks grew louder and she realized the door between cars had slid open. Heart racing, she craned her neck to look and saw the older woman exit the car. Now they were alone except for a man sleeping at the very back of the car.

The door closed, muffling the sound of the tracks, and Nick coaxed her onto his lap. "What are you doing?" she asked, even as she settled onto his leg.

"I wanted to be able to reach you better." He slid his hand beneath her skirt once more and nudged her thighs apart. Gently, he explored the folds of her clit, using her own moisture to lubricate the sensitive nub. As he began to stroke her, he lowered his head once more and suckled her breast.

She fought to hold back against the onslaught of sensation, to prolong the ecstasy. She was dimly aware of the ridge of his erection against her hip, and the way the motion of the train forced them together, then farther apart. He was panting, this evidence of his need tearing at her own control.

He sucked hard on her nipple, sending her over the edge. She bit her knuckle to keep from crying out as she came, rocking against him, held secure by his encircling arm. She collapsed against him, eyes closed, his hand cupped between her legs in a gesture that was both tender and possessive.

He nuzzled at her neck and kissed her jaw. "My turn," he said.

She smiled, and reached down to grasp him through the open zipper of his jeans, feeling his heat seep into her palm through the thin cotton of his briefs.

He sagged back against the seat and looked up at her. "Choose your weapon."

She pulled down his boxers enough to expose his erection, and cradled it in both hands. The easiest thing would be to jerk him off with her hands. That was probably what he was expecting. But why not take advantage of the darkness and privacy to enjoy something more?

She slid off his lap and stood before him, then bent and grasped the waistband of his jeans. "Raise your butt," she whispered.

"What? Why?"

"Just do it. I'm going to pull down your pants."

He did as she asked, and before he could ask any more questions she straddled his thighs, spreading her skirt over and around him. She slid up until the length of his shaft pressed against her clit. "What are you doing?" he asked.

"This." She stood, spreading her legs wide and fumbling under the skirt to guide him into her. It took several tries to find the correct angle, but she forced herself to relax and in a moment, he slid in.

She moaned softly as he filled her, and experimented with a few thrusts. By standing on tiptoe, then lowering her heels, she could achieve a satisfactory rhythm. Nick grasped her hips and guided her, arching up to meet her each time she stood flat-footed.

The rocking of the train established their rhythm, the sway of the cars forcing them together, then pulling them apart. She put her hands on his shoulders and closed her eyes, striving to rise up higher on her heels and to lower herself over him with more force.

His fingers dug into her hip, and his breath came in a series of huffing pants in time with the churn of the train engine. She felt the tension in him tighten and release as she thrust forward, and threw her arms around him to pull him close. Their movements gradually slowed until they were scarcely rocking together, letting the train's sway replace any effort on their part.

She would have stayed like that for hours, their arms around each other, their bodies as close as they could be. But they'd be coming to the end of the tunnel soon, and the stop for Winter Park was right after that. She didn't want to be caught quite literally with his pants down.

Reluctantly, she eased off of him, and pulled a handful of tissue from her purse to clean herself. Nick pulled up and zipped his pants, and then she curled up beside him, his arm around her shoulder, her head resting against his. Later she'd go downstairs to the washroom and clean up, but for now she wanted to savor the moment.

Alone in the semidarkness, partners in the slightly naughty, slightly risky game, she felt closer to Nick than she had ever felt to anyone. She'd taken a different kind of risk today, trusting him with this secret side of herself, and he hadn't questioned or tried to change her.

She didn't always understand what drove her to do some of the things she did—whether it was fear or joy or determination not to waste her second chance. Nick didn't seem to feel that he had to understand, either. He let her be herself and didn't question, a gift he probably didn't even realize he was giving her.

THE TWO LOVERS napped for part of the afternoon, then shared lunch in the dining car while the open country of western Colorado passed outside the window. They found seats in the observation car on the side overlooking the river and marveled at the occasional glimpses of white water or colorful rafts full of tourists.

As promised, Glenwood Canyon was spectacular, with marbled cliffs towering above the Colorado River. When the train pulled into the Glenwood Springs station a short while later, they were met by a van from the Hotel Colorado and driven the short distance to the historic inn.

"What should we do first?" Lexie asked, dropping her bag on the bed in their third-floor room. "Maybe a dip in the hot springs?"

Nick shook his head. "Time to go to work." He opened the desk drawer and pulled out the telephone book and tossed it to her. "Call every Bowman listed and see if you can get a lead on our man."

She sat on the edge of the bed and began flipping through the phone book. "What are you going to do?"

He pulled out his cell phone. "I'm going to let the rental car company know they can deliver our car. Then it'll be time for some legwork."

When he hung up the phone again, Lexie was sitting cross-legged on the bed, her skirt arranged over herknees. "No Oliver Bowman in the directory," she said. "No Bowman of any kind."

"It was a long shot, since we didn't turn up anything before. But he could still be here, unlisted or under another name."

"So where do you start to look?"

"People tend to do the same kind of work even when they change identities because that's what they're trained for and what they're drawn to. Bowman worked at auto body shops, so I'll visit anyone who might have employed him in this area. And they tend to have the same habits. Bowman liked to drink a few beers after work. He went to the same place every day. So it's worth checking out the local taverns."

"We should divide up the list," she said. "I can visit any places within walking distance of the hotel."

"All right. But if you spot him, don't say anything. Call me and we'll talk to him together."

"It's a deal."

Twenty minutes later he set out in a rental car for West Glenwood Springs. His first stop was Bud's Body Shop, a two-bay shop situated between a used furniture store and an air-conditioning service company.

The office was empty when he walked in, so he went on through to the shop, where he found a burly young guy with a shaved head spreading Bondo on the fender of a Ford Explorer. He straightened when he saw Nick. "What do you need?" he asked.

"I'm looking for a guy who might work here, or maybe he worked here at one time." He took the snapshot Oliver's sister had given him and offered it to the mechanic, whose coveralls were marked with the name Mac.

Mac wiped his hand on his coveralls and took the picture. "So what are you looking for him for?"

Typical response. Most people assumed he was a collection agent or a cop. "His family hired me to find him. He could be in line for a substantial inheritance." Not exactly a lie. He had no idea if Oliver Bowman would ever inherit anything or not.

"Oh, yeah?" Mac took a closer look at the photo, then handed it back to Nick. "Sorry, I haven't seen him."

The story was the same at four other body shops, an

automobile dealer and two bars. Nick was nursing a beer at a third bar when his cell phone rang.

"I'm not sure, but I think I've found him," Lexie said, her voice low.

"Where are you?"

"A place near the corner of Eighth and Grand, Club Rocco. I walked in and there he was, having a beer at the bar."

"I'll be there in a few minutes. In the meantime, don't let him leave."

"What am I supposed to do if he tries to leave?"

"Distract him. Strike up a conversation. You'll think of something. If he does leave, get his license plate number."

"Okay. But hurry."

LEXIE SAT AT A TABLE near the door and sipped a rum and Coke, watching Oliver Bowman—or the man she *thought* was Oliver Bowman—out of the corner of her eye. This guy was the right age, about fifty, and had the same mousy brown hair, wire-rimmed glasses and hooked nose as the man in the picture Susan Trenton had given them. He was wearing dirty jeans, a denim shirt and scuffed work boots, as if he'd just come from work.

The regulars seemed to know him, nodding in greeting as they came into the little tavern, exchanging small talk as they passed on their way to feed quarters into the jukebox.

"How you doing down there, Bud? You ready for another?" The bartender turned her attention from the TV mounted in the corner and addressed the man at the end of the bar.

"Thanks, Tammy, but you know two's my limit. As soon as I finish this one I'll be heading to the house."

Lexie checked the door. No sign of Nick. And there wasn't much beer left in Bud/Oliver's glass. Any minute now he'd be getting off that bar stool and walking out the door.

Her stomach churned and she downed the rest of her drink. She fluffed her hair, wet her lips, then stood and made her way to the jukebox. She wished she'd worn a shorter skirt. Anything to command the man's attention. She studied the selections on the jukebox, stalling, hoping Nick would walk in.

The scrape of Bud/Oliver's glass on the bar as he slid it away from him was like a shriek in Lexie's ears. She whirled around and saw her quarry pushing away from the bar. Desperate, she lurched forward, colliding with him.

"I'm so sorry," she said, clutching at his shoulders as she fought to steady herself. She smiled and looked him in the eye. He had milky blue eyes, his expression unsuspecting, slightly confused. "I'm so clumsy," she said. "It's these new heels." She looked down at the platform espadrilles, which were not terribly new, but she hoped he wouldn't notice. The whole point was to draw attention to her legs—to get and hold his attention until Nick arrived.

"That's okay," he said. "No harm done."

"Let me buy you a drink," she offered.

He shook his head. "Thanks, but I'm done."

He started to move past her, but she reached out and took hold of his arm, angling her body to block his path to the door. He'd have to shove her aside to leave now. She smiled, hoping the warm look would keep him from being too suspicious. "Then maybe you could buy *me* a drink."

She thought for a minute he was going to turn her down, but he relented, and settled back onto the bar stool. She sat beside him, nearest the door. "What'll you have?" he asked.

"Rum and Coke, thank you."

Tammy brought the drink, raising one eyebrow in question at Bud/Oliver. He shrugged. Lexie sipped the drink, then turned to him. "My name's Lexie," she said. "Short for Alexandra."

"I'm Bud."

Oka-aay. So he wasn't much for conversation. She tried again. "Do you live here in Glenwood, or are you visiting like me?"

"I live here."

She decided to adopt the persona of an overly chatty female, hoping a sheer volume of words would coax more information out of him. "I'm here with my boyfriend," she said. "He's on business and I got bored waiting around the hotel all day so I decided to come down here and have a drink. I mean, in a bar you can always find somebody to talk to, right?"

He nodded, looking at the bar, not her. She couldn't decide if he was shy, or merely uninterested. She tried again. "So how long have you lived here?"

"About three years."

His answer sent a shiver through her. "I'm from Denver. I can't imagine living in a small town like this. I mean, what do you do here?"

"There's a lot to do," he said. "Especially if you like the outdoors."

"Where did you live before you came here?"

"I lived in Denver, too. But I didn't like it."

This bit of personal information gave her hope. Maybe

she was getting somewhere. "Why not? Denver's a great city."

He shook his head. "Too big for me." He shrugged. "But then, I'm not much for crowds. I like to be alone." He looked at her then, his eyes serious. Was he trying to tell her something? That if she were trying to pick him up, she was wasting her time?

"So why Glenwood Springs?" she asked.

"I always liked the place. One day I just decided to move here."

She sipped her drink. "Do you have any family here?"

"No. Just me."

It sounded like a lonely way to live to her, but he didn't seem particularly unhappy. She was beginning to like him. Despite his reserve, he was easy to be with. She could see why his sister missed him.

The door opened and Nick walked in. He stood for a minute, silhouetted in the doorway, his broad shoulders and erect posture setting him apart from the other patrons even though he was dressed casually in jeans and an oxford shirt. He nodded to Lexie and walked toward her. "Hello there," he said, stopping beside her.

He turned to the man beside her and offered his hand. "Hello, Oliver," he said. "I've been looking for you."

Lexie watched as "Bud" stared at Nick's outstretched hand. His eyes held a panicked look and she knew then they'd found the man they'd been looking for.

12

THAT EVENING AT THE HOTEL, Nick watched TV in bed while Lexie, propped on pillows beside him, flipped through the pages of a magazine. Nick listened to the flutter of pages while he tried to concentrate on the news. No way could she be reading that fast. He switched off the television and rolled over to face her. "Okay, spill. What's wrong?"

She glanced at him, then looked back at the magazine. "What makes you think something's wrong?"

"You've got an expression on your face like you ate a sour pickle and you haven't said three words in a row since we got back from the bar this afternoon."

She tossed the magazine aside. "I just don't understand how Oliver Bowman can refuse to see his sister. She didn't seem like a bad person."

"He didn't say she was. But he apparently has no interest in seeing her."

"But she's his *sister*. His only relative. And she wants to see him." She looked at him, her eyes clouded with sadness. "How can he be so cruel?"

"He obviously doesn't see it as cruel. He just wants to be left alone."

Bowman's exact words had been: "I've left my old life behind and I don't see any need to go back."

"You can't shut yourself off from people that way," Lexie said. "Especially family. It's not healthy."

"He said he came here to start his life over. I can understand that." Wasn't that what Nick had done when he'd come to Denver—cut ties with the past, wiped the slate clean? Whatever cliché you used, it added up to the same thing—he was trying to live a different way, to avoid the mistakes of the past.

"I know all about starting over," she said. "But you can't do it by forgetting the past. The past is a part of you. You can't turn your back on it."

"Why not?"

"Because if you do, you're turning your back on part of yourself. The past is what made you what you are today. Why would you want to forget that?"

He frowned. "Maybe he has bad memories. Things we don't know anything about."

She shook her head. "If you try to forget pain, it's still there. It just gets buried, and then it sneaks up to hurt you even more some time later."

He sat up and rested his elbows on his bent knees, not looking at her. "And you know all this how?" He couldn't keep the sharpness from his voice. She might know a lot about physical pain, but she didn't know jack about emotional hurts. What was wrong with leaving behind reminders of that kind of pain—places that made you think of old loves, people who reminded you of successes that had turned into failures?

She leaned toward him. "After I had my accident, I refused to go anywhere near the place where it happened.

I'd go miles out my way to avoid that road and that curve where my car went off. Every time I'd get in the car, I'd tense up, remembering. For a while I even stopped driving. But in a city with limited public transportation, that didn't work. And I knew I couldn't keep asking friends for rides. So one day I gutted it up and made myself drive out to that curve."

"So? You got back on the horse and rode it again. Good for you. What does that have to do with Bowman?" *Or with me?*

"When I drove to that curve again I was able to see exactly what happened. I understood what went wrong. And I knew what to do so it wouldn't happen again. I think it's like that with all the things that hurt us."

He shook his head. "I don't think you're right. That curve is always there, always the same. People aren't like that. They're going to react in a different way almost every time you see them. You can't predict that."

"You can't," she agreed. "But you can change the way *you* respond to them. It takes time, but you can do it. But not if you don't stay around to face them."

He hunched his shoulders, trying to ease some of the tension knotting his muscles. "What's this 'you'? We're talking about Bowman, not me."

"Of course we are." She sat up straight again. "I was just saying… If things aren't right between him and his sister, he ought to take the opportunity to make them right. She's reaching out to him."

He sighed. That was the trouble with women. They focused too much on *feelings* and emotions. They'd be better off if they looked at situations from a logical aspect. "We can't make him take it. We left him her address and phone number. Maybe one day he'll change his mind."

"What will you tell her?"

"I'll tell her we contacted him and he doesn't want to be found."

She plucked at the coverlet between her knees. "Will you tell her where?"

He hesitated. The kindest thing would be to lie and tell her their search had come up dry. But that wasn't what Susan Trenton was paying him for. "I'll tell her he's living in Glenwood Springs under another name. That I don't have an address for him or know anything more. That I talked to him in a bar and I'm convinced it really was him. That's as much as I know."

"So if she wants to come here and try to find him herself she can?"

He nodded. "She can do that, but I wouldn't recommend it."

"Why not?"

"Because if he tells her the same thing he told us, it's going to hurt."

"She's hurting now. And he might feel differently once he sees her."

He shrugged. "Maybe so." Maybe things would work out for Susan and her brother. As for him, he didn't see any profit in revisiting the past.

He watched Lexie as she got out of bed and went into the bathroom, the hem of her negligee barely covering her bottom. He felt himself stir at the sight.

"Do something for me while you're in there."

She paused in the doorway. "What's that?"

"Take off that scarf."

Her hand went to her throat and there was no mistaking the fear in her eyes. "Why?"

"Because it doesn't look like it would be comfortable to sleep in." He sat up and leaned toward her. "Because I'm tired of not knowing what's under there." His voice softened, weariness creeping in. "Because it's been a rough day and I want one good thing to come from it."

She stood there a moment, watching him, her hand still at her throat. Then she whirled and went into the bathroom, shutting the door behind her.

He collapsed back on the bed and stared up at the ceiling. So much for expecting her to trust him by now. He should have kept his mouth shut. At least then he'd have a good chance of getting laid. Between Oliver Bowman's stubbornness and his own big mouth he was liable to end up sleeping on the floor the rest of the trip.

He just needed…something more from Lexie right now. Some part of their relationship that went beyond the physical. A guy could get by with superficial stuff only so long. You made a physical connection with a person, you wanted more. Some emotional tie.

He covered his eyes with his hands. All this thinking made his head hurt. He was tired of thinking. Of talking.

In her current philosophical mode, Lexie would probably accuse him of avoiding problems. And why not? He'd been doing pretty good with that approach so far.

But being with Lexie had led him to one unsettling conclusion: he wasn't so sure anymore that living a life completely different from the one he'd lived before was going to keep him from getting hurt again.

LEXIE STOOD IN FRONT of the bathroom mirror, studying the three-inch vertical slash, puckered and faintly purple against the skin of her throat. *No big deal,* Candace had said.

People will hardly notice, her doctor had assured her.

But *she* noticed. To her the scar was like a brand, a constant reminder that she'd made a mistake that had almost cost her everything.

She looked toward the closed bathroom door. Nick was waiting. Could she walk out there, naked in a way she'd never been before with him?

His request wasn't unreasonable. It wasn't even surprising. Before leaving on the trip she'd even told herself she would find some appropriate time this weekend to reveal herself to him. Maybe at the pool. Or some evening.

But in none of the scenarios she'd played out in her imagination had Nick *asked* to see the scar. The request unnerved her. It took the moment out of her control and made it mean more than she wanted.

She glanced at the mirror again, then at the scarf lying limp beside the sink. She could pick it up, put it back on, go out there and refuse to discuss the matter further.

But if she did that, there would be a new distance between them, an invisible barrier thin as the silk of the scarf and as impenetrable as stainless steel.

She took a deep breath, and opened the door.

Nick was lying on the bed, one hand over his eyes. She thought at first he was asleep, but when she moved toward him he stirred. He shoved up onto his elbows and watched her approach. "You took off the scarf," he said when she stopped beside the bed.

She nodded.

"Thanks." He sat up, and reached out to touch her, his fingers brushing across the scar. "It's not ugly at all," he said. "It's just another part of you."

She was afraid she might cry, so she put her hands on

his shoulders and pushed him back down on the bed, then straddled him, her thighs squeezing his sides.

He caressed her hips. "You're beautiful," he said. "With or without that scarf."

"It's not really a matter of vanity." Not totally, though there was some of that. "I just don't like looking at it and being reminded."

"Then we'd better do something to take your mind off of it now." He slipped his hands beneath her gown and hooked his fingers into the elastic of her panties. She took the hint and helped him take them off of her, then set about undressing him.

She was surprised at how hard he was, how ready for her. "Me losing the scarf was a real turn-on for you, wasn't it?" she said, shaping both hands to his erection and smoothing down it, like a potter shaping clay.

"More like the idea that you'd do that for me was a turn-on." He captured her face in his hands and kissed her, mouth open, tongue thrusting, claiming her.

The sudden strength of her own desire stole her breath. When she began to feel dizzy she remembered to exhale. He shoved her gown up until it was around her neck, and began licking and suckling her nipples. She tore off the gown and tossed it over her head, then gave herself up to the pleasure of his mouth on her. Every pull of his mouth resonated all the way to her clit, which throbbed to the mantra running through her brain, *I want, I want, I want.*

She smoothed her hand down his back, smiling at the familiar pleasure of her palm sliding over each indentation of his spine. There was something to be said for knowing your lover's body well—the places that gave you pleasure, the places that pleasured him. Two strangers could never satisfy each other the way two people familiar with each other's curves and quirks could.

He began kissing her throat, each feather brush of lips and tongue sending tremors through her. When he planted his mouth over the scar tears filled her eyes. She was close to losing it—bawling like a baby in his arms.

She shut her eyes tightly and forced her mind away from such dangerous thoughts, focusing instead on the physical—the slightly rough feel of his chest hair rubbing against her sensitive nipples, the hard arc of his rib cage beneath her hand, the rigid heat of his erection, the growing dampness between her thighs.

She pulled his head up and kissed him—a fierce, insistent kiss. At the same time she reached between them and began to stroke his penis. She wanted to channel the intensity she was feeling into hard and fast sex—until physical sensation overwhelmed emotion. She didn't want to think about what she was feeling or what any of it meant. She only wanted the release of joining her body with Nick's, of feeling his arms and legs wrapped around her.

He grasped her waist and rolled them over onto their sides, then rolled again so that she was on her back, looking up at him, into dark eyes that seemed to see past the surface to the innermost part of her. The idea both frightened and thrilled her, and fed the need she had to be closer to him. "Take me now," she breathed. "I don't want to wait."

"Then we won't wait."

He entered her easily, sinking deeply and filling her completely. She shut her eyes and rolled her head back, thrusting against him, wanting to squeeze every bit of pleasure possible from this moment.

She grasped his hips and urged him to move faster, each thrust deeper. Desire drove her, every other thought or sensation overwhelmed by need. "Yes," she breathed each time he filled her. "Yes. Yes. Yes."

Her climax was sudden and intense, white light exploding behind her closed eyes, white heat spreading throughout her body. His release soon followed and they continued to rock together for some minutes, then he collapsed on top of her, his elbows on either side of her ribs taking most of his weight off of her, though his head rested heavy on her shoulder.

She cradled him, idly smoothing her fingers through his hair. She felt burned clean by the encounter, more relaxed than she could remember being.

Was it because she'd finally trusted him enough to show him her scar? Or because he'd asked to see it in the first place? Or merely because today of all days, when the encounter with Oliver Bowman had confused and depressed her, she didn't have to be alone. She was with someone who knew her and accepted her. Someone who tried to understand.

How many people in this world could say the same? How many people were that fortunate? Did Oliver Bowman have someone here with whom he shared that kind of bond? Or was he a determined loner, unwilling to give up any part of himself to another?

Nick rolled off of her and lay beside her on the bed, one hand at her throat, resting beside the scar. His eyes were still closed. She wondered if he even noticed where his hand lay, or had any inkling of what it meant to her to be touched there.

When she'd first met Nick, she'd never imagined she'd ever feel as close to him as she did now. It was an exhilarating, scary feeling, as thrilling and frightening as any free fall from a plane must be.

But there was no need to panic. She still had plenty of time to pull the rip cord and release her parachute and drift to safety.

But first, she'd enjoy the ride a little while longer.

LEXIE MANAGED to shake off her frustration with Oliver's narrow-minded decision to turn his back on his sister and focused on enjoying the rest of their stay in the resort city. For the next two days, she and Nick swam in the famous hot springs, rode bikes through the canyon and visited Glenwood Caverns. They made love in the antique four-poster bed in their hotel room and slept in each other's arms. The interlude away from the city had a honeymoon quality, though Lexie refused to allow herself to think of it that way. After all, she and Nick were good friends, but neither of them were looking for anything permanent. Playing the "what if?" game would only get in the way of enjoying each moment together as much as possible.

But after three days devoted to pleasure, the routine of an ordinary workweek was something of a letdown. Monday afternoon, Lexie found herself sitting at her desk, studying the little red book that held her list, reviewing her accomplishments and considering the things she hadn't yet achieved. The trip to Glenwood Springs had allowed her to check off numbers forty-seven and fifty-one on her list—making love on a train and making love in a public place. She figured the train counted for both. But there were still so many things she hadn't gotten around to yet.

Her gaze landed on number forty-five, travel to Spain.

Her deadline for that one was fast approaching. Her Spanish class ended in three weeks and though she hadn't shown any real talent for the language, she felt competent enough to ask directions or order in a restaurant without embarrassing herself. She'd applied for a passport and collected brochures from a travel agent, but had stalled out on actually making her reservations. What was holding her back?

The door opened and a weary-looking Nick came in. His tie was loosened and his jacket was draped over his arm. "It's warm out there today," he said, tossing the jacket onto the coat rack in the corner.

"How did it go with Ms. Trenton?" Lexie asked. Nick had decided to deliver the bad news to his client in person.

The lines around his eyes deepened and he shook his head. "She was pretty upset. Pissed at me."

"She's really angry at her brother, but he's not around to yell at."

"I told her she was free to go to Glenwood Springs and try herself. I even gave her the name of the bar."

"Is she going to go?"

"I don't know. Maybe. I hope it works out for her."

"I hope it works out for them both."

"Anything come up while I was gone?"

"You have an appointment tomorrow with a Dan Ventura from Imari Industries." She flipped open the schedule on the corner of the desk. "At ten o'clock."

He studied the entry in the schedule. "Did he say what he wanted?"

"No. Just that he wanted to discuss hiring you."

"We can always use more business." He nodded to the red book opened in front of her. "Checking off more items on your list?"

She shrugged. "A few. And trying to decide what to do next."

"Anything you need help with?" He grinned.

She directed her gaze to the ceiling, though she couldn't hold back a small smile. He'd certainly been a great deal of help so far. "You never know."

He leaned over the desk and she caught a whiff of his aftershave, spicy and clean. She'd never smell that scent again without thinking of them together. Naked. "Mind if I take a look?"

She shook her head to clear it of the erotic image. She leaned back to allow him access to the book. "Go right ahead." After all, they'd shared so much already. Why not give him this peek at her dreams?

He scanned the list, then put his finger on number forty-five. "That's coming up pretty soon, isn't it?"

She smoothed the ends of the scarf around her neck. "I don't have an exact date yet."

He straightened and moved around to the other side of the desk. "Don't be in any hurry on my account."

Her heart beat a little faster at his words and she looked up, her gaze intent on him. "What do you mean?"

He picked up a stack of mail and began to sort through it. "Just that I think things have worked out well for us so far. You're going to be a hard act for anyone to follow."

Her heart felt as if a giant hand squeezed it. She was sure he meant the words as a compliment, but did they mean he was already thinking about replacing her? Not that they hadn't planned on this all along, but at the time she hadn't imagined it would hurt so much to think of him with someone else.

She pushed back from the desk and stood. "I think I'll

walk down the street and get something cold to drink. Do you want anything?" The thing to do was to not think about Spain or leaving or anything else right now.

"No thanks." He tossed a sheaf of mail into the trash and gathered up the rest. "I'll be in my office if you need me."

She grabbed up her purse and set out for the convenience store on the corner, focusing on the feel of the July sun on her shoulders and the sounds of her heels on the pavement. Candace had accused her of looking ahead too much, but now she saw the value of living in the moment. When the time came, she'd deal with finding someone to take her place in Nick's office, if not in his bed. But that time wasn't now.

DAN VENTURA turned out to be a short, worried man with a big problem. "Imari Industries manufacturers high-end cosmetics," he explained as he sat across from Nick's desk the next morning. "You may have heard of our Imari brand."

"I'm not that familiar with cosmetics," Nick said. "How is it you think I can help you?"

Ventura rubbed his hands up and down his thighs, then reached up to adjust his glasses. "The cosmetics business is highly competitive. We're up against dozens of other companies for the dollars of women who are looking for the next miracle in a jar. Today it's not enough for cosmetics to offer attractive colors and long-lasting coverage. Consumers are looking for products that fight aging, repair damage and protect against harmful sunlight and environmental hazards. Our work is as much about chemistry as it is about color and our formulations are absolutely top secret." He leaned toward Nick, his face pinched and anxious. "Someone has been stealing our secret formulas. A friend of mine, Stan Wittier, recommended you as someone who could help us find the person responsible."

"How do you know the formulas have been stolen?"

"We constantly monitor our competition. Recently, one of our chief rivals, Jackson Laboratories, released new products that precisely mimic one of our bestselling lines. By lowering their price temporarily and launching an intense advertising campaign they could effectively destroy the market for our products."

"Do you have any idea who might be leaking the formulas?"

He sat back, anxiety replaced by weariness. "None at all. We're a fairly small company and we have certain safeguards to protect the formulas, but obviously someone has breached those barriers."

"Why not go to the police?" It was a question he often asked. The answer often revealed much about the client's personality and motives.

Ventura's face paled. "The last thing we want is public knowledge that this is happening. It could lead stockholders to unload all their shares and result in a total collapse of the business."

Nick sat back in his chair and considered the situation. "I'd need access to everyone in the company, and it would probably be best if they didn't know who I really was or why I was there."

Ventura nodded. "Of course."

"You could say you'd hired me as a new employee. Perhaps a temporary or contract worker."

"I suppose that could work. We sometimes hire temporary labor for help with seasonal workloads."

"You'll also have to tolerate my snooping around on all levels. I'll include a non-disclosure clause in my contract, promising I won't reveal any sensitive information I find regarding your work."

Ventura compressed his lips into a thin line. "I suppose that can't be avoided."

Nick opened his file drawer and took out a new client packet, with rate sheets and the necessary paperwork. "You may want to take this and review it."

"No, I don't want to wait any longer. We can't let this problem go on. Tell me where to sign."

"All right." Nick pointed out areas on the contract that needed Ventura's initials or signature.

"You'll start right away?" Ventura asked.

"Tomorrow, if you like."

"Absolutely." Ventura stood. "I can't stress how important this is."

"You've put yourself in good hands." He stood also and shook hands with his new client. "In cases like these often an outside eye can spot irregularities you may be too busy or too close to see."

"I hope you're right."

Nick escorted Ventura to the front door, then stopped off at Lexie's desk to give her the contract. "And what does Mr. Ventura need you to do?" she asked, pulling out a file folder and neatly labeling it for the contract.

"Someone's stealing trade secrets. I'm going to go undercover at his place as a temporary worker and see what I can snoop out."

She laughed. "You? A temp?"

"What's wrong with that?"

"You look as much like a temp worker as I do a cop."

She looked him up and down. "No offense, but a guilty person would suspect you after one look."

He straightened his tie and buttoned his jacket. "Why do you say that?"

"How often were you asked to go undercover when you were with the police force?"

"I didn't do undercover work."

"So they never used you for any kind of special assignment or sting operation or anything."

He shook his head. It was true that street cops were sometimes asked to pose as students or johns or other roles in various situations, but he'd never done that kind of work.

"Maybe that's because everything about you screams 'cop.'" She stood and walked around him, as if inspecting for some flaw. "Tall, broad-shouldered, short hair, clean shaven, flinty-eyed." She laughed. "You could be a recruiting poster."

"I'll dress down. Grow a beard. Wear glasses." He frowned at her, exasperated. "I'll slump."

"Or you could let me do the job."

"You? You don't have any training. And what if you were caught? There's a lot of money at stake here, and when money's involved, that means the situation could be dangerous."

"I don't have to have special training to spot someone who's behaving suspiciously. And I look exactly the way people expect a temporary office worker to look. In fact, I've done temp work, so I know what to expect, how to act. I can report to you with anything unusual and you can advise me what to do next."

He shook his head. "I don't like it. You could get hurt."

"I won't get hurt if nobody knows the real reason I'm there. And they won't find out." Her eyes met his, refusing to look away.

He shoved down an unfamiliar anxiety, passing it off as annoyance at having her horn in on what was, after all, *his* job. He'd gotten used to working alone. Did she expect him to just hand over the reins of a major case like this?

"You'll still be in charge," she said, correctly sensing the reason for his hesitation. "Think of me as your eyes and ears in the company."

He nodded. Anyone else, he would have immediately said no, but he knew Lexie was smart, not over-emotional or given to foolish behavior. And she was probably right about her being more suited for the role of office worker than he was. Hell, he could scarcely type, and the thought of days spent in a windowless office, filing forms and making copies, made him break out in a rash.

"I'd have to have access to the offices, too," he said. "And a cover story that would allow me to come and go freely, so I could take a closer look at anything you found."

Her smile widened. "That's easy. You can pose as my boyfriend. No one will think twice if you bring me to work or stop by for lunch or pick me up in the evenings."

He might have pointed out that he already was her boyfriend, after a fashion. Though what did you call a relationship begun primarily for sex that had moved on to friendship, or even something more that both of them avoided even mentioning? "All right. I think that will work. There's only one other problem I see."

"What's that?"

He looked around the office. "What am I going to do without you here?"

"I can still stop by to catch up on any urgent office work in the evenings. And I could probably work weekends."

"That's too much. What if you worked part-time at Imari Industries? Say, three days there and two days here?"

She nodded. "If you think that will be enough."

"We can vary your days, so no one knows for sure when you'll be in. That might help us catch the culprit off guard."

"It's perfect."

"I'll call Ventura and set it all up. Then I'll go over all the details with you. You'll need to start tomorrow."

"I can't wait. Thanks, Nick. I won't let you down, I promise." The joy on her face made his chest hurt. God, she was beautiful. And it killed him to think how much he was going to miss her when she was gone.

13

ON LEXIE'S FIRST MORNING posing as a temp, she met the
principals of Imari Industries. In addition to Dan Ventura,
there was Andrew Jeppson, a very tall, very thin man who
shook hands with Lexie as if he feared he might catch some
germ. She would have bet money he washed his hands as
soon as she was out of sight. The third partner was Mac
Emerson, a stocky man with the build of a truck driver and
the demeanor of a kindergarten teacher. He put Lexie at
ease right away. "I hope you'll enjoy working here," he
said when she and Ventura stopped by his office. "We like
to think of ourselves as a very egalitarian bunch, so if you
need anything, don't hesitate to ask me or anyone else for
help."

"Thank you," she said, trying not to stare at the floor-
to-ceiling display of knives, swords and machetes on the
wall behind him. "I'll remember that."

"Kind of takes your breath away the first time you see
it, doesn't it?" Emerson said, nodding toward the display.
"It's my pride and joy."

"Mac collects knives," Ventura said, though he didn't
look too thrilled with the idea.

"Not just knives—any bladed weapon. Mostly military
issue, though I have a few novelty pieces." He picked up

a long slender blade she'd assumed was a letter opener from the corner of his desk. "This bayonet dates from 1861. I'm starting to focus on Civil War pieces. It's an exciting market."

"Maybe you can show her the rest of the collection another time," Ventura said, backing toward the door. "We'd better get back to work now."

"He's certainly very friendly," Lexie said as Ventura led her down the hall to the warren of cubicles where she'd be working.

"Mac is the public face of Imari Industries," Ventura said. "Not the brightest bulb in the building, but a born salesman, and really charming if you don't get him off on the subject of his knife collection."

"It looked like a huge collection to me. Does he have more at home?"

Ventura shrugged. "He's in a pretty small place right now. The most valuable pieces are in his office, I'm sure. He said he wanted to take advantage of our security system."

"Where do you and Mr. Jeppson come in?" she asked. "No offense, but it seems odd to me that a company that makes cosmetics for women is run by three men."

"Not so odd, really. The three of us were suite-mates in college. We always talked about going into some kind of business together. Andrew is a very talented chemist. He started out developing soap and disinfectants, but hit upon a formula that proved to have amazing restorative powers for the skin."

"So Andrew creates the products and Mac sells them. What do you do?"

"I'm the businessman. I'm the one who makes it all come together and work."

"And you're the one who first became suspicious about the competition's new line of products?"

He nodded. "I track the market very carefully. I immediately noticed the similarity in Jackson Lab's claims and ours. But I wasn't certain anything untoward was happening until I purchased some of their products and had them analyzed by an independent lab."

"They were similar?"

"Enough that I knew someone had leaked our proprietary formulas."

"Why hire an independent lab? Why not test the other products here?"

He glanced at her out of the corner of his eyes. "I didn't want to alarm anyone here until I was sure. Plus, an independent analysis makes better evidence in court, should we decide to sue."

"Will you sue?"

"That hasn't been decided. That may depend on your findings."

She thought the answer was curious. Did Ventura suspect one of his partners of giving—or perhaps selling—the secret formulas? It would explain his reluctance to involve the police or the courts.

"You'll be working with our clerical supervisor, Mindy. Mindy, this is Lexie, our new temp." Ventura introduced her to a plump thirtysomething woman who appeared to be wearing the full Imari line of cosmetics, including purple glitter eyeshadow and dark red lipstick.

"Hey there," Mindy said, scarcely glancing at Lexie. Her attitude clearly said she couldn't be bothered getting to know someone who wouldn't be around for the long-term. "You can start with the filing. It's been backing up since the last temp left."

Lexie felt queasy at the sight of the five-foot-high stack of papers waiting to be filed that teetered in a corner of the closet-sized file room. She could be stuck in here for days, away from all the action. She'd have to take numerous breaks to go to the restroom or for a drink from the water fountain if she was going to see anything more than files A through Z.

"Invoices in these cabinets, purchase orders over here, correspondence here and the others drawers are labeled for any categories I haven't mentioned." Mindy pointed out the various sections in the ranks of filing cabinets. "Any questions?"

"Whatever happened to the paperless office?"

Mindy frowned and shook her head, then left Lexie to filing hell.

Sighing, she slipped on a rubber thumb and prepared to do battle with the column of papers. This was probably as good a place as any to get an overview of Imari Industries' operations. If she spotted anything suspicious, she could check it out further.

Half an hour later, she was resorting to pinching herself to stay awake. The various invoices, orders and memos she'd encountered so far were as interesting to read as the tax code. She sneaked a peek at a few toward the bottom of the pile and they dated back to 1999. Perhaps the previous temp had died of boredom before she could complete the task.

When her phone rang she almost cried in relief and lunged for it. Nick's number flashed on the screen. "Did you call to rescue me from this hellish drudgery?" she asked.

"That bad, huh? What do they have you doing?"

"Filing." She looked around the cramped room. "I'm stuck in a closet, away from everyone and everything. Not exactly a prime spying position."

"Take advantage of it. Forget the papers. Check out the files."

"I was going to do that." Well, it probably *would* have occurred to her, eventually. "What are you doing?"

"Surveillance on a guy who filed a suspicious worker's comp claim."

"Did you see anything interesting yet?"

"He's got a wife *and* a mistress. Anybody that active can't be hurt too badly. He doesn't strike me as too bright, so I'll probably get something incriminating before the day's out."

"Do you have someone in here with you?" Mindy appeared in the doorway of the file room.

"I'm on the phone," Lexie said.

"We don't allow personal calls during business hours," Mindy said, her frown spoiled by the severely upward arch of her penciled-in brows.

"I'll only be a moment." Lexie turned away from her. After all, it wasn't as if she was likely to be fired. Maybe insubordination was one way to get transferred to another, more interesting department.

"Who is that?" Nick asked.

"That's Mindy," she said. "My supervisor."

"She sounds like a lot of fun."

"Speaking of fun, I can't *wait* to see you again." She lowered her voice to a seductive purr, deliberately provocative. "It's been way too long, tiger."

Out of the corner of her eye she saw Mindy's mouth drop open, then snap shut.

"Tiger?" Nick laughed. "Can't you do better than that?"

"You're a tiger in bed. And you make me purr." The line was so cheesy, she could hardly get it out, but Mindy was appalled enough to make tsking sounds and turn on her heel.

"I'd like to make you purr all right." Nick lowered his voice to a growl. "But I'd rather make you scream."

She swallowed hard, a rush of heat between her legs. "She's gone now," she said. "No doubt to file a report about the new temp having phone sex in the file closet."

"Sounds interesting. Tell me more."

"I'd better go," she said, even though the idea of experimenting with dirty talk with Nick held far more appeal than facing the never-ending files. "I'll talk to you later."

"Definitely."

She hung up the phone, smiling to herself. No telling what Mindy thought of her now, but why not have a little fun mixed with her work?

Unfortunately, by the end of her first week on the job, all hope of fun had faded. She'd succeeded in escaping the file room on the second day by stashing the last three feet of paperwork that dated back five years in empty file folders in the bottom drawer of the "Miscellaneous" file cabinet. To her way of thinking, the papers were technically filed, and who was going to look up five-year-old purchase orders and inventory sheets anyway?

When she informed Mindy she was done and Mindy verified this with a brief tour of the file room, she was promoted to making copies, a task which allowed her to roam the offices freely. Except for posters of an elegant-looking model with slightly Asian features—"the face of Imari"—posted throughout the building, the office was as dull as any other she'd ever been in. While Imari Industries' products were glamorous, the job of producing them held almost no excitement. To keep herself alert and amused, she'd resorted to shocking Mindy with gushing references to her boyfriend, the Tiger, and their various sexual exploits. The older woman listened with a mixture of horror and fascination to Lexie's ever-wilder tales.

Unfortunately, with Nick stuck doing surveillance for much of the days she worked at his office, and Lexie juggling two jobs, classes and other obligations, there had been more action in Lexie's imagination than in reality. By Friday she was restless and edgy, missing Nick's body *and* his mind. She wanted a chance to have more than a brief phone conversation about the case. Maybe his experienced eye would see something in the Imari Industries offices that she'd been missing.

So when he volunteered to pick her up from work on Friday, she jumped at the chance. "Come right at five," she said. "Everyone should be pretty much cleared out by then and you can take a look around."

"Will Mindy be there?"

"Probably. She's usually one of the last to leave."

"Then I'll do my best to be as amorous as she believes."

Promptly at five, Nick cleared security and rode the elevator up to collect Lexie. She had to bite the inside of her cheek to keep from laughing when he appeared dressed in tight black jeans, a silk shirt unbuttoned to midchest, hair slicked back in a pompadour and gold-rimmed sunglasses. "Hey, kitten," he said, greeting her with a kiss that might have passed for mouth-to-mouth resuscitation.

Mindy, purse in hand, showed up just in time to see the

back-bending finale of the greeting. She stared, open-mouthed, hand on her chest.

"You must be Mindy." In Mr. Suave mode, Nick took her hand and kissed it, sending a flush of red up her neck and face. "Lexie's told me so much about you."

"N-nice to meet you," Mindy stammered.

"I won't keep you," he said, walking her to the door. "But I'm so glad we had the chance to meet."

Still looking dazed, she walked out the door. A few seconds later, they heard the elevator open and close. Lexie collapsed against a desk, her whole body shaking with laughter. "I don't believe it," she gasped between giggles. "You're so incredibly cheesy."

He whipped off the sunglasses and tucked them in his shirt pocket. "I wanted to prove to you that I *could* go undercover. No one would mistake me for a cop now."

She nodded. "I hope not. Did you see the look on her face? She's shell-shocked."

"I wanted to get her out of here before she could start asking questions." He looked around. "Is everyone else gone?"

She nodded. "The doors automatically lock and you can't get in without a pass code, unless someone lets you in."

"Good." He grabbed her hand and pulled her toward the back of the office. "Come on. Show me the layout of this place and we'll see what we can find."

"First, you've got to see this." She led him to Mac Emerson's office. Though the door was locked now, they could see through the glass window that opened onto the rest of the office. "Take a look at the back wall," she said.

Nick whistled. "Knives?"

"He's a collector. Don't dare ask him about it, or he'll talk your ear off."

Nick took another look. "Pretty big collection. I wonder if it's valuable."

"He says it is. Mr. Ventura says he keeps it here because the office has a security system and his home doesn't."

"I guess when you're as rich as these guys must be, you have to spend money on something." They continued on their tour of the offices.

"Who's the babe?" Nick asked, when they stopped by the break room. A life-size cutout of the model holding a vial of some face-saving serum smiled at them from the corner by the microwave.

"'The face of Imari.' I think her real name is Giselle, or something like that. You know, one of those fashion models with only one name."

Nick studied the cutout, then shook his head. "She doesn't do much for me." He winked at Lexie.

She laughed, enjoying the pleasant warmth that spread through her. It was good to be with a man who could make you laugh *and* feel sexy. "The only place I can't show you is the lab," she said, leading the way out of the break room. "It's off-limits to everyone but Andrew Jeppson and his team."

"Are the formulas kept there?"

"Dan Ventura says only portions of formulas are revealed to lab workers. Jeppson knows them, of course, since he's involved in developing them. Ventura says he's seen some, though they don't really mean anything to someone without a scientific background."

"What's this Jeppson character like?"

She shrugged. "Not the friendliest guy in the world, that's for sure. I get the impression he relates more to his laboratory equipment than he does people."

"Maybe he's holding a grudge against the world. Or maybe just his partners. Revenge could motivate someone to sell out his partners."

"Maybe. So you think Jeppson is our man?"

"I don't know. Is he the only one who knows and understands the complete formulas?"

"There are copies in a safety deposit box to which each of the three partners have a key."

"So Jeppson, Ventura and Emerson are suspects. But anyone who had access to the deposit box key could also obtain the formulas."

"But who has access to the key?" Lexie asked. "I don't think it's something that would be kept here at the offices."

"A family member or lover of one of the partners might know where the key is kept. Or a trusted secretary."

Lexie shook her head. "That's a lot of people. Can't we narrow it down any?"

Nick leaned back against a desk and folded his arms, his brow furrowed in concentration. "We could look for anyone at Imari Industries who also has a tie to Jackson Labs. And we could look for anyone who would have a motive to sell the formulas to the competition."

"They wouldn't necessarily have sold the formulas. Maybe they gave them away. Or maybe Jackson Labs has a spy here who stole the formulas."

"Maybe. But I have a hunch money is involved. It usually is in situations like this."

She slumped into a desk chair and put her chin in her hands. "Great. I don't even know where to begin to look."

He straightened. "Back to your favorite place. The file room."

She made a face. "Why there?"

"I want to see the personnel files."

"That cabinet is kept locked."

"That won't slow us down much."

Lexie led the way to the file room and showed Nick the drawers containing personnel records. He examined the lock, then straightened out a safety pin and worked it into the mechanisms. In a matter of seconds it popped open. He pulled out a stack of files and handed them to her. "We're looking for anyone who is a former employee of Jackson Labs. Also any notations of anyone who's had their wages garnished for taxes, child support, anything like that. Any signs of financial difficulty."

They made quick work of the fifty or so employee files. Lexie found no one who had worked for Jackson Labs and no clue that pointed to an employee in financial difficulty. "Anything strike you as unusual about these files?" Nick asked when they'd looked through them all.

"Everyone's worked here a long time," she said. "Mindy's the newest person here and she's been here five years."

Nick closed the file drawer and shook his head. "I'm not sure we're going to come up with anything like this. We'd do better in the lab, but I doubt either one of us could pass for a scientist."

"I almost blew up the chemistry lab at my high school," she said.

"I forgot everything they taught us as soon as the test was over," Nick said.

"So what do we do now?"

He looked at her. "I'm open to suggestions."

She gave him a wicked grin. "Oh, I have a few suggestions." She wrapped her arms around his neck and leaned against him, her face tilted up to his. "They don't have anything to do with the case, however."

He slid both hands down to cup her bottom and snugged her more tightly against him. "I've missed you," he said.

She wriggled against him, sliding along the erection the tight jeans did little to conceal. "I've missed you, too."

They kissed, his lips warm and insistent on hers. She responded with the fervor of an unrepentant hedonist, reveling in the taste of his mouth, in the feel of her breasts pressed against his chest. In the short time they'd known one another, he'd learned her so well; he knew exactly how much pressure to apply with his lips, where to place his tongue, when to tease her with gentle suction. She could have kissed him for hours, until their lips were numb and her head was spinning, if not for the heat and tension growing as the rest of her body demanded attention.

"Let's get out of here," he said, his lips scarcely leaving hers, his hand kneading her buttock.

"We don't have to leave yet." She brought one leg up to wrap around his hip, trapping him against her.

"We're not going to find anything else here today." He caressed the length of her naked thigh. His gaze locked to hers, his eyes dark with lust. "I've waited all week to be with you. I don't want to wait any longer than I have to."

"We don't have to wait." She kissed the V of his chest where his shirt fell open. "I spent a lot of time in this room thinking about you."

"You did?"

"I had to do something to keep from going crazy from

boredom." She grinned and unfastened another button on his shirt. "I never knew a file room could be so sexy before."

"Anywhere you are is sexy." He kissed her again, and slid his hand higher up her leg, and around her inner thigh. His fingers slipped easily beneath the lace edge of her panties. "You're very wet," he said, smiling against her mouth.

"I told you this room was sexy."

"I don't think it has anything to do with the room." He slid one finger between her slick folds, covering the pulsing head of her clit, pressing down. She gasped and arched against him. His smile broadened. "I think I've found the magic button."

"I want you," she said. "Now."

He walked them back until she was pressed against the closed door. With his right hand still between her legs, he used his left hand to shove her shirt up to her neck and popped the catch on her bra.

She closed her eyes and pressed her head back against the door, abandoning herself to a torrent of sensation. He spread her own wetness across her clit and began to stroke back and forth with his finger, building the tension.

He transferred his attention to her other breast, and reached down to unfasten his pants and free his erection. She took him in her hand, the feel of his hot, heavy shaft arousing her further still.

She was anxious now, focused on her impending climax, surrendering to him and to the power of these feelings between them. A low moan tore through her and her whole body shook when she came. Then, while her muscles were still contracting and releasing, he hiked her skirt up higher and slid into her, crouching slightly to achieve the proper angle, his powerful thighs supporting them both.

His thrusts slammed her back against the door, rattling the file cabinets on either side. The urgency of his need gripped her. She clutched at his shoulders and encouraged him to go deeper still. "Don't stop," she gasped, each stroke reverberating through her like the bass notes of a song, felt as much as heard. "Please don't stop."

An animal groan tore from his throat as he came. He thrust again and again until he was spent, then moved his hands up her thighs to her waist, letting her slide to the ground as he moved out of her.

They stood with their heads together, leaning on each other and the door, their breath ragged pants, hearts thudding. "You make me crazy, you know that?" he said after a while, his voice hoarse.

"I do?" She brushed back his hair and looked into his eyes. "Is that good or bad?"

He shook his head. "I don't know. I'm supposed to be a professional but I don't act like one with you."

She grinned. "You're a pro when it comes to making love to me."

"You're no amateur yourself." He brought the halves of her bra together and fastened them, a tender gesture that brought an unexpected lump to her throat.

She swallowed hard. "Maybe I'm just a fast learner."

"You are that." He pulled her shirt down over her bra and looked into her eyes, his gaze intense, searching. "Don't you realize there are people who would think it was unethical for me to be having an affair with you?"

She pulled down her skirt, uncomfortable by this serious turn of conversation. "Why is that?"

"Because you're my employee." He pulled up his

pants and tucked in his shirt. "They'd say I'm taking advantage of you."

"Only because I let you." She reached down and pulled up the zipper on his pants. "Maybe *I'm* taking advantage of *you.*"

"That might be closer to the truth." He ran his hand through his hair. "I'm obviously unable to resist you."

"You don't seem to be trying too hard." She gave him a coy look and smoothed her hands up his chest. This was what she was more comfortable with—flirting and teasing. She didn't want serious talk after sex.

He stepped back, out of her reach. "No, I'm not. I don't know what that says about me."

She folded her arms over her chest and frowned at him. "Why are we having this conversation now, after all this time?"

He looked around the file room, at the rows of labeled drawers and boxes of supplies on the shelves along one wall. "Maybe it's being here, in this office, where people don't normally do things like this."

"How do you know? They may be boinking each other on the desks when no one's looking."

He looked at her, the seriousness of his expression erasing her attempt at levity. "Maybe it's because I know you're going away soon, to Spain or wherever. And I wonder what the time we've spent together means."

"Why does it have to mean anything?" Why couldn't he let them *be* without having to worry about heavy stuff like meaning?

"I don't know. But shouldn't it?"

"It means we had a wonderful time. You'll always be special to me."

"But not special enough for you to stay."

His words hit her like a weighted exercise ball, suddenly tossed in her direction. She stared at him, throat tightening. "Do you want me to stay?"

He looked away. "I don't know. That's something you have to decide on your own."

What was going on here? Two minutes ago she'd been elated to be in his arms again. Now she felt this incredible sadness. And he looked utterly miserable. "I—I'm not going away because I don't want to be with you anymore," she stammered. "It's just…I have so many things I haven't done yet. So many places I haven't seen."

He turned away. "I know. Forget I said anything."

How could she forget? And how could she end the conversation on this depressing note? She took a step toward him. "Maybe…you could come with me?"

He shook his head. "No. My life's been too unsettled these past two years as it is. I want to stay put for a while."

And she'd spent too many years staying in one place, her life not going anywhere. "I'm sorry." She wrapped her arms around herself, as if she could squeeze out the ache in her heart. Why did she have to choose like this? Why couldn't she have Nick and the other experiences she craved?

He turned back toward her. "Look, let's just forget it." He put the sunglasses on. "We agreed in the beginning we would have a good time. And that's what we've done. I'm just frustrated by the investigation, that's all."

She nodded. "Right. We won't talk about it anymore." What was to be gained by talking, anyway? Much as she liked Nick—much as she loved him, even—she was too afraid of what would happen if she tried to stay with him. She couldn't let herself become complacent and stale, the way she had before the accident. She'd struggled too much to get healthy again to go back to her old life. If she stopped learning and striving and experiencing new things and called herself content with the status quo, that would be as bad as dying all over again.

They finished dressing and started to leave the file room. Nick's hand froze on the door. "What is it?" she asked.

"Shhh." He tilted his head, listening. "Do you hear that?"

She listened. Her heart pounded as she heard the scrape of a chair on the floor, and then footsteps approaching the door.

Nick's eyes met hers, dark and wary. "Get behind me," he whispered. He stepped in front of her just as the knob turned and the door to the file room opened.

14

NICK'S POLICE TRAINING always kicked in at moments like this. His eyes searched the file room for possible weapons and escape routes while his brain manufactured several glib explanations to toss at whoever was on the other side of the door. His adrenaline ran high, though logic told him the situation was likely to be more embarrassing than dangerous. Still, if the person opening the door was the one they were looking for, and he or she had figured out what they were up to…

Mac Emerson peered around the edge of the door, his expression wary. His gaze flickered from Nick to Lexie and back to Nick again. "I thought I heard noises in here," he said. "What are you two up to?"

Nick opened his mouth to speak, but Lexie stepped in front of him. "Oh, Mr. Emerson, I'm so embarrassed," she said, lashes fluttering, cheeks bright pink with what might pass for a blush to anyone who hadn't just seen her in the throes of passion. "I had no idea anyone was still around to hear us."

"To hear you doing what?" Emerson opened the door all the way now. Nick was startled to see that he was holding a huge knife. The blade was at least a foot long. He put a protective arm around Lexie, not ready to trust the grandfatherly businessman.

Lexie looked at the ground and hugged her arms under her chest, effectively accenting her cleavage. Emerson's eyes immediately zeroed in on her chest. Nick bit back a grin. Lexie definitely had methods of distraction at her disposal that he lacked. "It's just that my boyfriend and I have both been working so much, we've hardly seen each other lately and I was showing him around the office and we came in here and started kissing and…"

"And one thing led to another." Nick hugged her close and assumed his best smarmy demeanor. "Sorry, man, but Lexie here's just so irresistible, you know?"

Emerson frowned, but at least he'd stopped holding the knife like a sword, instead letting the blade drop to his side. "I don't have to tell you that's very unprofessional behavior," he said.

"I know. And I'm sorry." Lexie looked convincingly contrite. "I promise it won't happen again."

"See that it doesn't." He held the door open wider, a clear signal that he expected them to leave now.

Lexie ignored the gesture. "What are you doing here so late, Mr. Emerson?"

"As one of the leaders of Imari Industries I often have to burn the midnight oil," he said. "Being vice president of a company isn't all about a corner office and perks, you know."

"Of course." She smiled, a look that could have melted butter. "But you really shouldn't work so hard."

"I don't mind. I thrive on it, really." He motioned toward the exit. "You two had better go now."

"That's a wicked knife," Nick said, nodding to the blade as he and Lexie moved past.

Emerson brandished the blade again. "It's a Civil War side knife. I picked it up recently and I'm thinking of selling it. I was actually on my way here to look up the original invoice when I heard you two."

"Lexie tells me you have quite a knife collection."

"Yes. It's a fascinating hobby."

"I always wanted to do something like that." Nick shrugged. "Too expensive for me, though."

"Some of the finer pieces can cost tens of thousands of dollars." His eyes narrowed and his mouth turned down in a scowl. "And I'll have you know a very expensive alarm system protects my collection."

Nick raised both hands in a gesture of innocence. "Hey, you don't have to worry about me, dude."

"Come on, tiger, let's go." Lexie took his arm and led him toward the door. "Good night, Mr. Emerson. Thanks for being so understanding."

Nick waited until they were in the elevator on their way down to the lobby before he said anything. "Why did you tell him we'd been having sex in the file room?" he asked.

She shrugged. "I figure the best policy is to tell the truth whenever possible."

Right. Except telling the truth—or attempting to do so—hadn't gotten him very far with her.

He shoved his hands in his pockets, fighting the black mood that threatened, forcing his mind to focus on the case. "Do you buy Emerson's story about coming to the file room to look up the invoice for that knife?"

The elevator opened and she led the way out and across the lobby. "Maybe," she said when they were on the sidewalk out front. "Or maybe he heard the noises and grabbed the knife to use as a weapon in case it turned out to be a burglar."

He nodded. "That collection of his must be worth a

small fortune." He was definitely going to take a closer look at Mac Emerson.

If nothing else, work would help keep his mind off Lexie and his confusing feelings for her.

"Now, WHEN DO YOU think you'd like to begin your trip?"

"Um, I'm not sure. Maybe four weeks from now?" Lexie sat at the travel agent's desk, brochures for trips to Spain spread out before her. *"Beautiful España!"* one proclaimed against a background of Moorish architecture. She'd planned for this trip for so long, but now that she was actually making reservations, the butterflies she felt had nothing to do with excitement.

"And how long did you want to stay?" the travel agent asked.

"I'm not sure. I was hoping to decide that after I'm over there."

The agent frowned. "We can do an open return, but you understand it's more expensive?"

"I understand."

The agent typed into her computer and frowned at the screen. "I can get you on British Airways to London Heathrow, with a connecting flight on Iberia Airlines to Seville departing August fifteenth."

"That sounds fine." She glanced at the calendar mounted on the wall beside the agent's desk. August fifteenth was only three and a half weeks away. That wasn't very long, was it? She'd have to put an ad in the paper right away to find someone to take her place at the detective agency. Her stomach knotted at the thought.

"Do you need a hotel or rental car? Or would you like to sign up for a tour?"

She probably ought to think about all those things, but she wasn't ready for that yet. "You can arrange accommodations through the tourist desk once you arrive in the country, can't you?"

"Yes, but you won't have any way of knowing ahead of time what kind of rooms are available or where they are."

"That's okay. I don't mind surprises." That's what this trip was all about, right? She wanted to be spontaneous and follow her imagination wherever it would take her, unrestricted by any itinerary or convention.

"The price is three thousand, six hundred and sixty-eight dollars. You'll have to pay today to guarantee this reservation."

"All right." She fumbled in her purse until she found her charge card and handed it over. Maybe after she'd spent a few weeks in Spain she'd come back to Denver and look up Nick again. They could start over, with an eye toward a more permanent type of relationship. Not that she wanted to rush into anything, but there was something to be said for sticking with one man for a while. Maybe she'd been a little hasty when she'd decided she ought to sleep with six different men before she turned thirty. Maybe one really interesting man was enough.

"Will this be just you, or do you have a traveling companion?"

"Oh. It's just me. I'm traveling by myself." The thought had never bothered her before, but now it sounded lonely. Did the agent think she had no friends to go with her? That she was antisocial? "I plan on meeting people in Spain," she said. New people, but for all the agent knew she was getting together with childhood friends.

The agent ran her charge card through the machine and returned it to her, along with the charge slip. "If you'll sign this please, I'll go to the back and get your ticket off the printer."

While the agent was gone, Lexie checked her watch. Twenty minutes before she had to be back at work at Imari Industries. How much longer was Nick going to keep her there before he called it quits? They hadn't been able to come up with anything overly suspicious about the people who worked at the company. Nick said both Mac Emerson and Andrew Jeppson's finances were a mess, but he could say the same about half the people in Denver, couldn't he? That didn't mean they'd turned to crime. And why sabotage their own company?

"Here you go." The agent returned and handed Lexie a fat envelope. "All your tickets and transfers are there. You'll need to show up at the airport at least two hours before your flight."

She nodded and stuffed the envelope in her purse. "Thank you."

"Let me know if you decide you need a hotel or want to sign up for a tour. We have some very nice specials."

"I'll remember that."

She left the travel agency and walked briskly up the block to the high-rise where Imari Industries occupied the seventh and eighth floors. She was scarcely at her desk before Dan Ventura came to see her. "Nick said he thought it would be a good idea if you checked out the lab," he said, leaning close so that no one around them could make out their conversation.

She nodded. "That would be great." Though unless she spotted someone with a copy of the secret formulas hanging out of his back pocket, she doubted it would be much good. Still, it was better than sitting here typing letters while Mindy repainted her nails shocking pink.

The Imari Labs were located one floor up, through a series of locked doors and security checkpoints. Dan flashed his ID and was waved through, Lexie trailing in his wake. Outside the lab itself she was issued a long lab coat, paper booties and a paper hair covering. "We don't want any outside dust or dirt contaminating the products under development or skewing test results," Ventura explained as he donned his own protective garb.

Three technicians, including Andrew Jeppson, were working at computers when they entered. Lexie was disappointed not to see an array of test tubes and Bunsen burners. "This isn't where they make the prototypes?" she asked.

"We make some prototypes here," Jeppson said, getting up from his desk and coming to greet them.

"We have a new product in development right now, don't we Andrew?" Ventura said.

Jeppson frowned. "We do."

Ventura led the way to a glass-front cabinet on the wall and opened the door. "How are the tests coming?" he asked.

"The preliminary round demonstrated good results," Jeppson said. "Better than expected, although it's too early to ascertain if these results will be consistent over time."

Ventura held up a glass jar that contained a pale pink cream. "This is our newest product. It's a cover-up that hides almost any blemish or scar, while at the same time fading the scar or eliminating the blemish. Initial test results have shown it works on even old scars and birthmarks. Stretch marks, burns, surgical scars—it can hide and in some cases eventually eliminate all of them."

Lexie ran one finger under the edge of the scarf around her neck. Though she was willing to take it off when she and Nick were alone now, she hadn't yet worked up the nerve to bare her neck in public. Could that simple-looking cream really cover and even fade her tracheotomy scar? She wouldn't hesitate to pay almost any price if she thought it would really work.

"We don't know that for sure." Jeppson took the jar from his partner and replaced it in the cabinet. He turned to Lexie. "We're still testing."

"Scientists are bred to be cautious," Ventura said. "While businessmen like me know success requires risk." He looked at Jeppson. "It's going to work. And it's going to be our biggest moneymaker yet."

Jeppson nodded, though he was still frowning at Lexie. Was he bothered by her intrusion into his work, or did he suspect the real reason she was here? Was he worried she'd find something to incriminate him?

Ventura led Lexie away, showing her the various sections of the lab, nodding to the two other technicians, who glanced at Lexie, then turned back to their work. She didn't know whether she should be insulted at the snub or impressed by their dedication. "Each technician knows only one part of the formulation," Ventura explained. "Only Andrew knows the whole thing, and he's the only one with access to his computer."

"What would happen if he died or were injured in an accident?" she asked.

"There are codes in the safe that would allow the other partners to access the information we'd need." He led her out of the lab to the changing room, where they stripped off the caps, coats and booties and deposited them in hampers.

"And the three of you have been friends since college?" she asked.

"Andrew and Mac actually knew each other in high school. I ended up rooming with them in college. Andrew was the geek, Mac was the jock and I was somewhere in between." He shook his head. "The same roles we all play now, after a fashion."

"Mac isn't exactly a jock."

He laughed. "No. But he has that jock mentality—great personality, but he never had a head for math or science. In fact, he barely graduated. But he can charm anyone, a great quality for a salesman."

"Are you worried someone will steal the formula for your new product?" she asked when they were in the elevator on their way back to the business office.

"Yes. That's why I hired Nick to help us." His eyes met hers. "You haven't found anyone, have you?"

She shook her head. "Who do you suspect?"

"I don't know. I don't want to suspect anyone." He shook his head. "It's a small company. We've all been together a long time. It hurts to think there's someone I've trusted who has betrayed everything we've worked so hard for."

The elevator opened and they stepped off into the hallway outside the business office. Lexie stared at the "face of Imari" poster that filled one wall of the foyer.

"Do you know who that is?" Ventura asked.

She shrugged. "Not really. Someone said her name is Giselle."

"That's the name she uses for work. She's also the former Mrs. Mac Emerson."

She blinked, waiting for this information to sink in.

"Mac was married to *her?*" She couldn't picture this elegant woman with the stocky, knife-loving Mac Emerson.

"Hard to believe, I know, but it's true." Ventura looked up at the huge smiling face. "I told you Mac can be very charming. And I don't suppose it hurt that he was worth a great deal of money at the time."

"They're divorced now?"

He nodded. "She hired a very good lawyer and ended up taking Mac to the cleaners. She got a piece of everything he owned."

"Everything?"

"Except the knives. She hated those. I wondered sometimes if that's why he took up the hobby in the first place."

She stared up at the slogan at the bottom of the poster: *Don't let your past be a predictor of your future.* She wondered now at the wisdom of this advice. Maybe it was important now to take a closer look at the past, to see what clues she could find there for what was playing out now.

THE DOOR BUZZER sounded and Nick looked up to see the mail carrier deposit a stack of mail on the corner of Lexie's desk. Lexie was working at Imari today and the office was empty without her. Even the phone had been silent, as if people knew she wasn't here to answer it.

He shoved out of his chair and went to sort through the mail, standing over the trash as he did so. Junk, junk, ad, bill, junk, bill, junk, letter…

He turned the small padded envelope over and read the return address—1432 Magnolia Place, Houston, Texas. He blinked and read it again, just to be sure he'd gotten it right. That was his old house in Houston. His ex-wife's place now.

He picked up a letter opener and slit the flap, then

shook out the contents of the little packet. A square leather folder slid into his palm, followed by a scrap of paper. "Found this while cleaning closets. Thought you might want it. M."

He opened the folder and time stopped as he stared at the picture of his younger self looking back at him. He was wearing a brand-new uniform, his hat cocked over hair clipped too short and the beginnings of a goofy grin lurking just on the edge of what was supposed to be a stern scowl.

His first badge—from when he was a probationary officer, fresh from the police academy. He leaned back against the edge of the desk and stared at the laminated ID he'd received with such pride all those years ago. God, he'd just been a kid!

He glanced at the empty envelope on the desk beside him. He recognized Monica's handwriting now. What had she thought when she came across this? Was she annoyed because she thought she'd already rid herself of everything that was his?

Or was that anger gone from her, worn away by time and other events that were more important to her now? She must have mellowed some, if she'd gone to the trouble to send it to him.

For that matter, hadn't he mellowed, too? He didn't hate his ex-wife anymore. He didn't even hate what had happened. Hate was a sharper pain than the dull regret that still gnawed at him in some unguarded moments.

He studied the picture again, at the young man who'd been so sure of his future. Back then, he'd thought he knew exactly how everything would work out.

And almost nothing had turned out the way he'd

planned. The picture before him blurred and he shut his eyes tightly against the sudden tears. He was the good guy, dammit! He'd done everything he was supposed to do, played by all the rules. He'd gone to the Academy, become an officer and married his sergeant's daughter. He'd planned to put in his twenty years of service, collect his pension and retire to start a new business and enjoy his grandkids.

Then Monica had decided she wasn't happy with his plans and had made new plans of her own that didn't include him. He could still remember the cold feeling in his stomach when he realized he wasn't anybody special. His life wasn't golden. He was just another cop with a busted marriage, a failure who'd never failed at anything before.

Rather than go back to the force and face everyone knowing what had happened—not to mention put up with Monica's father glaring at him when he thought no one would see—he'd handed in his badge. He'd told himself he was doing it to save his marriage, but he was really trying to save his pride.

He opened his eyes again and took a deep breath, then shut the folder and laid it aside. Pride was about as over-rated as his certainty that he could chart his own course had been. Life just happened sometimes, and you went along for the ride.

One thing was for certain—you couldn't control other people. He hadn't been able to control Monica, and he couldn't control Lexie now.

Why had he said all that about her staying the other afternoon in the file room? Was it because he knew she was determined to leave and thus he didn't have to be afraid of her answer? After all, he'd gone into this thinking she was the safest kind of relationship—one that wasn't meant to last. If things had to be temporary between them, he would have a good time and avoid all the messy emotional stuff at the end.

He'd gotten good at lying to himself, so good he'd actually believed that bunk. At least for a while. But when she'd confirmed she still intended to leave, it had hurt more than he would have imagined. He thought he'd guarded his feelings well but they'd turned out to be wrapped in gauze.

So why hadn't he taken the next step and told her how he felt? Sure, it might not make any difference, but what if it did? What if he had a chance with her and blew it?

And why couldn't he get past his damned pride?

When Monica had left him, he'd told himself pride was all he had left, so he had to hang on to it, to prop himself up with it. But wasn't it time he let go of that crutch?

15

NICK RANG THE BELL at Imari Industries and waited for someone to buzz him through. "Who is it?" a woman's voice asked over the intercom.

"Nick Delaney. I'm here to see Lexie."

The woman giggled. "Sure, *tiger.* Come on in. She's in the mail room."

Great. Apparently word of his and Lexie's escapades in the file room had spread. Nothing like a little office gossip to attract attention. On the other hand, if people thought Lexie's main interest was in getting it on with him they wouldn't suspect she was snooping for dirt.

Too bad he *wasn't* her main interest. Not that he expected to be any woman's be-all and end-all, but it would be nice to think he ranked higher than, say, a trip to Spain.

"Nick! What a nice surprise." Lexie abandoned the mail trolley and rushed to greet him. She gave him an enthusiastic kiss. Sure, it was part of her role for this job, but that didn't mean he couldn't appreciate it. And if he held on to her a little longer than necessary, put it down to saying goodbye.

"What brings you here, tiger?" she asked, while half a dozen co-workers looked on.

"I stopped by to say goodbye, kitten," he said, doing his best to get into his role. "I have to go to Houston for a couple of days."

"Oh, no!" Her disappointment seemed genuine, but maybe she was merely a great actress. "Why?"

"I have some business to take care of. I'll be back tomorrow afternoon, or the next day at the latest."

She pouted. "I was counting on you to help me with a special project I'm working on." Her expression implied that the project was something risqué, but the sober look in her eyes told him she was referring to something at Imari.

"A new project?"

"Yes. Working here has really *inspired* me." She glanced around and the workers who had been watching them avidly made a show of getting back to work. "Learning the *history* of this company and the *people who started it* has really made me want to improve myself."

"Really?" What about the company's history and its founders had she learned? "I can't wait to hear all about it as soon as I get back."

She took his arm and walked him toward the door. "Let me go with you to the lobby so we can say a proper goodbye." As they passed her desk, she reached for her purse, but caught it by only one strap, spilling the contents across the desktop.

"What a mess," she said, scrambling to sweep keys, checkbook and assorted makeup back into the bag.

"Don't forget these." He bent and picked up a packet of papers that had slid to the floor. Turning the packet over, he saw the name of a travel agency stamped on the front. "What's this?"

"Those are my tickets to Spain." She snatched them

from his hand and stuffed them back into the purse, avoiding his gaze.

The words made him feel fifty pounds heavier. "I didn't realize you'd already made reservations."

"I did it at lunch yesterday." She settled the purse on her shoulder. "I was out running errands and saw the sign for the travel agency and thought, why not go ahead and do it?"

"When do you leave?"

"A little over three weeks." Her gaze met his, then darted away. "I was going to tell you as soon as I saw you again."

He nodded. Sure she was. And it wasn't like he hadn't known this was coming. But he'd been hoping to find a way to change her mind. That's part of what this trip to Houston was about. "So, did you get a good price?"

She shook her head. "Not really. I bought an unrestricted ticket and those are more expensive."

Could she find a way to make this worse? "You mean you don't know when you'll be coming back?"

She shrugged. "I haven't decided. I thought it would be good to get over there and just do what looked interesting, see whatever I felt like seeing. I mean, the whole point is to be spontaneous, experience new things and meet new people, right?"

New *men?* The thought made him queasy. He turned and headed toward the door. He heard her follow, the high heels of her sandals tapping on the tile floor. She caught up with him at the elevator. "Remember you asked me before about the woman in all the Imari ads?" she said, nodding to the oversize ad for Imari cosmetics that filled one wall of the foyer.

"Yeah. Some model with one name." The elevator opened and he stepped inside.

"She's Mac Emerson's ex-wife." She joined him in the elevator and punched the lobby button.

He blinked. "You're serious?"

She nodded. "At least according to Dan Ventura. Why would he lie about that?"

"That's interesting, but what does it have to do with our case?"

"According to Ventura, when they divorced she got 'a piece of everything'—except Mac's knife collection."

"Everything including the business?"

"I don't know, but I think we should find out, don't you? If she left him in financial straits, it might give him a motive to sell company secrets."

"I agree it's worth looking into, but don't do anything risky by yourself. Wait until I get back."

She nodded. "I won't do anything dangerous. I'll just poke around the office and see what I can find."

"Don't draw attention to yourself."

She laughed. "Too late for that. Apparently our fun in the file room garnered a lot of attention."

"So I realized when the receptionist called me 'tiger.'"

"It's not so bad, really," she said. "It could even work to our advantage. Now everybody thinks I'm just a dumb sex kitten." She flashed him a wicked grin. Any other time, the look would have had him contemplating stopping the elevator and trying for a repeat of their interlude in the file closet.

But his feelings for Lexie went beyond lust now. Too bad he'd only discovered this when she was on the verge of leaving.

The elevator opened and she followed him into the lobby. "Have a safe trip," she said, and leaned over and kissed his cheek.

"Yeah. Be careful while I'm gone."

She grinned. "Where's the fun in that?"

"I'm serious. Don't do anything reckless when it comes to this case."

She stood at attention and saluted. "I promise. I'll save that for when you get back." She winked. "Then we can be reckless together."

Laughing, she turned and raced back to the elevator. He fought the urge to run after her, to tell her to tear up that ticket to Spain and stay with him.

But she was the risk-taker in their relationship, not him. His days of being reckless were long past him, especially when it came to risking his heart.

LEXIE'S SMILE FADED as soon as the elevator doors shut. Despite her attempts to make light of the situation, Nick had seemed really down. Was he upset about this sudden trip to Houston, or because the case here at Imari wasn't going well—or about something else?

She hadn't missed the hurt in his eyes when he'd discovered she'd booked the trip to Spain. Sure, he'd said that the other night about hoping she might stay, but he'd seemed okay when she'd explained why she couldn't.

She'd thought *she'd* feel better about their situation once she'd bought the ticket, that taking the first step toward breaking things off with him would ease the burden on her heart. Instead, she'd spent a sleepless night and a distracted morning, trying to ignore the ache in her chest every time she thought of leaving Nick.

The elevator doors opened and she stepped out into the foyer of Imari Industries and looked up at the poster again. "Don't let your past determine your future," she read out loud.

Her own past was undistinguished by either great triumphs or great failures. Her life was like the glassy surface of a lake, reflecting nothing but placid sky. She'd traded her hopes for the humdrum, and hadn't really seen anything wrong until she'd awakened in that hospital bed. In those first days when she'd realized the enormity of what had happened to her, she wasn't so much afraid of dying as she was of never really having lived.

Going to Spain was part of her grand plan for living a better life. But now that she was poised to make the trip, all she could think of was how small and empty her life without Nick in it seemed.

"Lexie, what are you doing standing out here?"

She turned to find Mindy frowning at her from the doorway. "There's a ton of mail that needs to be distributed," her supervisor said. "And it's not going to get delivered by itself."

Lexie waited until she was past Mindy before she stuck out her tongue at the other woman's retreating back. One thing she absolutely wouldn't miss in Spain was the drudgery of temp work. And to think she'd pictured detective work as so exciting!

The day's mail included the usual assortment of invoices, advertisements and catalogs, as well as a fat padded envelope addressed to Mac Emerson. Lexie hefted the bulky package. Here was her perfect opportunity to try to learn more about Imari's affable salesman.

She saved Emerson's delivery for last and made sure

he was in his office before she approached. "Mr. Emerson?" She knocked on the frame of the open door. "I have a package for you."

He swivelled his chair around to face her, his expression coming to life when he spotted the package in her hand. "Yes! Exactly what I've been waiting for." He hurried forward to take it from her.

She made no move to leave, instead following him farther into the room. "The only time I get that excited is when I'm expecting a present," she said with a teasing look. "Is it your birthday?"

He laughed. "No, but I guess you could call this a present to myself." He picked up the bayonet that served as his letter opener and slit the envelope. "It's a new addition to my collection."

"Oh. A knife." In keeping with her bimbo persona, she allowed a little disappointment to show. "I'd rather have jewelry, myself."

"This is worth as much as a fine piece of jewelry." He pulled what, at first, looked like a wad of bubble wrap from the envelope and began to unwrap it. Finally he revealed a huge knife, easily a foot and a half long, with a wide, flat blade and a bone handle.

Lexie shivered. "It looks dangerous."

"In the wrong hands I suppose it could be." He grasped the hilt and held it out in front of him, admiring the burnished blade. "But to a connoisseur like me, this is a true work of art."

His eyes gleamed with an avarice akin to lust. Lexie wondered if he had an erection, but was too squeamish to look. Some things she didn't really care to know. "Is that knife worth a lot of money?" she asked.

"A bit. There's no point in collecting if you're not going to focus on the finest examples. Those that are most rare. Quality and scarcity combine to determine value, so those items that are of the highest quality, and are the most rare, command the highest prices. And of course the beauty of a collection like this is that it is always increasing in value."

"How long have you been collecting knives?" She turned to admire the wall of blades at the back of the office.

"Not long." He tested the blade against his thumb, drawing blood. She winced as he blotted the drops on a tissue. "Three years or so."

"Was your wife interested in collecting also?"

Her words effectively distracted him from the knife. He cut his gaze to her, eyes narrowed. "What do you know about my wife?"

She shrugged. "Someone told me you used to be married to the woman in the Imari ads."

He laid the knife atop the pile of bubble wrap. "At one time, yes. And, no, she was not interested in my collection."

"That's too bad." She gave him her most flirtatious smile. "I think it's really interesting. Very…masculine. And sexy." Amazing how smoothly she could lie when necessary. And what a strong gag reflex she had developed.

His shoulders relaxed a little, though his expression was still wary. "There are a few women collectors I've had the pleasure to meet."

That was it. Keep him talking. If he talked long enough, maybe he'd reveal something important. "How did you learn so much about it?"

"I attended shows, spoke with dealers, read extensively. Here—" he leaned back and picked up a stack of magazines from his desk "—these are trade publications dedicated to the serious collector. You may borrow them if you like."

The last thing she intended to do was waste her time thumbing through magazines, but she might as well let him think she was interested. "Thanks so much."

"Now if you'll excuse me, I have work to do, and I'm sure you do, too."

"Of course. And thanks again for the magazines." She backed out of the office and hurried to her desk, where she pulled a notebook out of her purse and began making notes.

1. Emerson didn't like the reference to his ex-wife.

2. If the knives he collected were so expensive, where was he getting the money to buy them? How much money was tied up in that collection anyway?

3. What was Nick doing in Houston? Did his visit have anything to do with his old life?

He'd never talked much about his past, but she knew that he'd been married before and that his ex still lived in Houston. Could that pinching at her heart at the thought of him going back to the city where he'd loved another woman possibly be…jealousy?

Where had *that* idea come from? She slapped the notebook shut and grabbed the top magazine off the stack and began flipping through it. She might as well see what the big deal was about all those knives in Emerson's office. Maybe she could find something in here that would tell her how much the collection was worth.

At the very least, reading an article or two might take her

mind off Nick. She flipped pages until the title of an article caught her eye: Cosmetics magnate specializes in Civil War weaponry. She sat up straighter, eyes opening wider as she began to read. Here was the information she'd been looking for—the details that could help them solve this case.

She grabbed the phone and punched in the number she'd memorized. One ring, two…after five rings an electronic voice said "The party you are trying to reach is unavailable. Please—"

She slammed down the phone and moaned in frustration. Dammit, where was Nick when she needed him?

NICK SAT IN THE RENTAL CAR across the street from the house, his hands slick with sweat as they gripped the steering wheel. The place looked pretty much the same as he remembered. Maybe the yard was greener—he'd never been much on yard work.

The curtain on the front window moved and he knew she was watching him. He'd better get out of the car and go on up to the door before she called the cops. Would anybody on the force still remember him?

The walk seemed half a mile long, though in reality it probably wasn't a hundred feet. She opened the door before he got there, a puzzled look on her face. "Nick? What are you doing here?"

"Hello, Monica." He stopped at the bottom of the front steps. She looked good. A few pounds heavier, maybe, but it suited her. She was wearing her hair differently; the style made her look younger. Or maybe being happy did that to a person. He realized with some shock that he really did hope she was happy.

"What do you want?" She kept one hand on the doorknob, ready to shut him out if she didn't like his answer.

"Thanks for sending the badge," he said. "I was glad to get it."

"I didn't see any reason for me to keep it."

Ah. There was the Monica he remembered, her words short and not always sweet. "Thanks all the same. I know you didn't have to send it."

"You didn't come all the way from Denver to thank me for mailing the badge."

"No." He sucked in a deep breath, shoved his hands in his pants pockets, then took them out again. He couldn't think of any smooth way to say what he needed to say, so he just laid it out for her. "I've been doing a lot of thinking and there's something I need to know from you. I need to know what I did wrong."

She leaned closer, studying him, confused. "What you did wrong?"

"With us. With our marriage. I know I screwed up, but how, exactly?"

She stepped back, half behind the door. "Is this some kind of joke?" She looked around, as if expecting a cameraman to pop out at any moment and yell *Surprise!* "Do you have some crazy idea you'll be able to fix things and we'll get back together?" She shook her head. "It's not going to happen. And did you forget I'm married to someone else now?"

"It's not a joke. And I know we're through." He straightened and looked her in the eyes. "I'm ready to move on. But I need to know what I did wrong. So maybe I can keep from making the same mistakes again."

She regarded him warily, chewing her bottom lip. "I told you all that when we split up," she said.

"Yeah." She'd told him a lot of things in those days, a tidal wave of words he'd let roll over him, anger and pain like wads of cotton in his ears. "But now I'm finally ready to listen."

She looked at him a long time, the tension going out of her expression. What did she see? he wondered. Did she see the man she'd once loved? Or the one she'd grown to loathe? Or someone more distant than that? Did she remember the good times, or only the bad?

At last she stepped back and opened the door wider. "Come on in. Eddie won't be home for another hour. We can talk."

He climbed the steps and followed her into the air-conditioned darkness of the house where he'd once lived, a place where even the scent hanging in the air had been familiar to him on those nights when he came home late and avoided turning on any lights for fear of disturbing her.

Now nothing looked or smelled familiar. Even Monica was different enough he might not have recognized her if she'd passed on the other side of the street. He almost smiled. For months he'd mourned the things he'd left behind, as if they were all here waiting for him and circumstance prevented him from enjoying them. He'd wasted all that time grieving for things that didn't even exist anymore, except maybe in his imagination.

16

WHEN MINDY DISCOVERED LEXIE sitting at her desk reading a magazine, she gave her a lecture on wasting company time, then assigned her to copy and collate agendas and handouts for the next morning's staff meeting.

Lexie scarcely heard the lecture, her mind too busy sorting out what she should do with the information she'd learned this afternoon. She was tempted to talk to Mac again, to see what he might add, but she remembered her promise to Nick to avoid taking risks.

Mac didn't look particularly dangerous, but he did collect knives, so she'd probably better play it safe and wait. If only Nick would hurry back to Denver.

The combination of extra work and a distracted mind meant she left Imari Industries later than usual. She hurried to her parking space on the roof of the garage and pulled her phone from her purse. She'd try to call Nick one more time before she headed home.

She made the call from her front seat, tapping impatiently on the steering wheel as she listened to the electronic ring. "The party you are trying to reach is unavailable. You will be forwarded to an automatic voice mailbox. Please leave a message at the tone."

"Nick, call me! It's important."

"Now what could be so important you have to talk to your boyfriend—or should I say your boss—right away?"

She gasped as Mac Emerson stepped up beside her car and pulled open the door. He was smiling the same open, welcoming grin with which he'd greeted her on her first day on the job, but in his right hand he held the massive Bowie knife, the blade polished to gleaming sharpness.

"Mr. Emerson, you startled me." She put her hand to her chest, doing her best to affect empty-headed surprise while she assessed the situation. He'd called Nick her boss. Did that mean he knew about the detective agency? Had he guessed the reason she was working at Imari?

She managed a lopsided grin, keeping her eyes on the knife. "Did you come to show me another new addition to your collection?"

"You ought to recognize this. It's the same knife you delivered to me this afternoon. Or were you so busy thinking about that detective boyfriend of yours you didn't notice?"

"Detective? Mr. Emerson, you must be thinking of someone else. Tiger's not a detective." So much for her policy of telling the truth. When her life was on the line, she was willing to lie through her teeth.

"Delaney Investigations. You're not the only one who can look into a person's background, you know."

"I don't know what you're talking about." She raised her chin and glared at him.

"A buddy at the bank told me your 'boyfriend' was snooping, asking questions about my accounts. I don't appreciate that." He grabbed her arm and yanked her from the car.

"Mr. Emerson, let me go!" She struggled to free herself

from his grasp, knocking over her purse in the process and spilling its contents across the seat.

Still holding her by the wrist, he leaned in and picked up a magazine that had slipped from her purse. He shook it out and frowned at the article it was open to, the one about the cosmetics executive who collected Civil War guns and knives.

"So you saw the article about Marcus Jackson," he said.

"When I saw the title, I thought it was going to be about you," she said truthfully.

"He's the one who used to own this knife." He admired the lengthy blade before holding it beneath her chin.

"Did you buy it from him?" she asked, trying to speak without moving her lips.

His smile broadened. "We made a trade. One that was advantageous for both of us." His eyes narrowed and his voice roughened. "You already figured that out, didn't you? Mindy complained about you goofing off all the time, but you were really snooping. And now you'll have to pay."

He tried to pull her across the garage, to the black pickup parked near the exit ramp.

"No. Help! Somebody help!" She screamed and kicked out at him, her cries dying in the stiff breeze that cut across the deserted rooftop.

"I wouldn't put up a fight if I were you." The blade he held to her throat was honed so fine she didn't feel it at first, until a trickle of wetness tickled her collarbone. She gasped, "You cut me!"

"Merely a scratch. I'll do much worse if you don't co-operate."

"Wh-what do you want?"

"I want you to come with me. We're going to go talk to your boyfriend." He began dragging her toward the truck again.

The elevator doors opened and a tall man in a white lab coat emerged. "Mr. Jeppson!" Lexie screamed. "Call 9-1-1."

Andrew Jeppson jumped and stared at them, eyes wide. He frowned. "Mac, what are you doing?"

"Get out of here, Drew. This is none of your business."

Jeppson hesitated, then turned and raced for the elevators again. "He's going to get help," she said. "You should let me go. We can say it was all a joke."

"He's not going to do anything. Drew is a man of science, not a man of action. Besides, he doesn't even know you. You don't mean anything to him, while I've been his friend for over fifteen years."

"What difference does that make?" she snapped, her initial terror waning, replaced by fury. How dare he do this!

"Drew knows the value of friendship. Geeks like him never have many real friends but even in high school, when I was the quarterback and the most popular guy in school, I let him hang out with me."

"Why? So he could do your homework for you?"

That remark earned her an angry scowl and another nick from the knife. Fresh blood ran down to soak her scarf. "Come on." He yanked open the driver's door of the truck and shoved her in. "Let's get out of here."

He climbed in after her, the point of the knife aimed at her side now. While he settled into the seat and turned the key in the ignition, she stared toward the elevator, willing it to open, willing Andrew Jeppson and help to reappear.

What if he hadn't called nine-one-one? What if he'd done what Mac had said, and simply left by another exit, willing, for the sake of friendship, to pretend he'd never seen anything in the garage?

Mac shifted into gear and steered the truck toward the exit ramp. Lexie searched for some avenue of escape.

She imagined she heard sirens, then sat up straighter, holding her breath as she listened to the wail grow stronger. She hoped it was the police headed this way, and not a single cop out to catch a speeder.

The sirens grew louder still, and more numerous. "Shit!"

Lexie stared at Mac, who was muttering curses under his breath, while cranking the steering wheel hard. "Drew must have called the police after all," she said. "If you leave me here and run, you can probably get away."

Not likely, but she wanted him to think it was worth a chance.

He reached out and grabbed her by the wrist, squeezing hard, bringing tears to her eyes. "What? Do you think I'm as dumb as the others make me out to be?"

She shrank back from him as far as she could and shook her head. "No. Of course not."

"They think I haven't heard their little jokes about the dumb jock." He shook his head in disgust. "But they're going to find out soon how smart I really am. Then I'll be the one laughing."

He stopped the truck near the elevators on the roof and switched off the engines. "What are you doing?" she asked as he rolled down the driver's side window and rested his elbow on the doorframe.

"We wait," he said. "And let them come to us."

NICK SLUMPED IN HIS SEAT on the return flight to Denver and stared out the window at the busy tarmac, seeing nothing. His mind was still trying to absorb what Monica had told him.

According to his ex, he was unemotional and closed-off. "You never told me how you felt about anything," she'd said. "You shut me out."

Is that how it had felt to her? He'd seen it as not burdening her with his problems or concerns. He'd thought he was protecting her.

The plane pushed back from the terminal and the flight attendant stood in the aisle and presented the safety demonstration. Too bad relationships didn't come with instructions like that—something to tell you what to do when things took a turn for the worse.

That's sort of what he had been looking for when he went to see Monica. He'd expected her to tell him he worked too many hours or he snored or forgot to take out the garbage one too many times. He hadn't anticipated she'd tell him he'd made her feel too alone.

"Flight attendants, prepare for takeoff."

He watched as the jet rose from the runway and lifted above the clouds. Roughly two hours from now he'd be back in Denver.

Is that how Lexie saw him, too? As someone who kept her at a distance? If that was the case, he couldn't even claim to be protecting her this time. More likely, he was protecting himself.

Until Monica had left him, he hadn't known it was possible to hurt that much. He'd thought by telling himself he wouldn't fall for Lexie he could keep from ever having to feel that bad again.

He wiped his hand across his face and grimaced. He'd have had better luck telling himself not to breathe. Somewhere between hiring her as his assistant and getting on that train with her at Union Station, he'd fallen in love with Lexie.

Being with her was like finding a part of himself he'd lost—the part that knew how to laugh and how to feel joy. Most people wouldn't consider that a bad trade-off, he supposed.

Only now she was leaving. For a different reason than Monica but the end result would be the same. Where would he run to this time to try to escape the hurt? He could go to Alaska or South America but he couldn't outrun himself.

Or he could try a different approach this time. He could stop being the close-mouthed tough guy and tell Lexie exactly what he was feeling. He could admit he loved her and ask her not to go.

The thought made his heart race. Could he even do it?

Sure, they were just words, but he'd rather face an armed gunman than lay his feelings bare that way. He knew how to defend himself against the gunman. He didn't have a clue how to fight back against emotional firepower. If Lexie rejected him, it would be worse than being shot.

But if he let her walk away without saying a word, that would be the worst kind of cowardice.

"Would you like to purchase a headset for use with our in-flight satellite television?" The flight attendant leaned into his row, gesturing toward the screen in his seat back.

"Sure." He leaned forward and pulled his wallet from his pocket. Anything for a distraction. "How much?"

"Five dollars, please."

He paid the money and accepted a pair of padded headphones, which he plugged into the jack on his armrest. Buttons on the armrest allowed him to select from sports, comedy and news shows. He settled for a broadcast of headline news, reasoning that an hour spent contemplating the world's troubles would help him to not freak out about his own.

"In developing news, police in Denver have responded to a hostage situation in a downtown parking lot. A man is holding a woman on the top level of a parking garage. The man is believed to be McKinley J. Emerson, one of three founding members of the Imari Industries cosmetics company. The woman has not yet been identified, but she is believed to be a temporary office worker. The reason for Emerson's attack on the woman has not yet been determined."

Nick stared at the images on the television screen, icy sweat forming on his brow. Mac Emerson was holding Lexie hostage? But why? Had she learned something incriminating about him? Was he the one selling company secrets to the competition and she'd found this out?

He punched off the station, then immediately switched it back on, afraid of what was going to happen to Lexie, but too afraid not to keep watching, in case of some new development in the story.

Hang on, Lexie, he thought as a picture of the Imari offices flashed on the screen. *Just hang on until I get there. Hang on.*

17

MAC BACKED THE TRUCK into position on the top floor of the garage, in the corner farthest from the ramp, but with a clear view of the approach. A concrete pillar protected him on one side, while the elevator bank partially blocked the other side. He rolled down both windows, letting in the heat that radiated off the concrete and the dirty oil smell of the garage itself.

The pillar blocked the passenger door, trapping Lexie between it and Mac. She glanced at the back sliding window, debating her chances of getting out that way.

"Don't even think about it," Mac said. He switched off the truck and eased the seat back. "It shouldn't be long now."

The wail of sirens seemed to surround them. She licked her lips, trying to get enough moisture into her mouth to speak. "What happens when the police show up?"

"We negotiate." He looked at her. "You in exchange for my freedom."

She started to shake, and clamped her teeth together to keep them from rattling. Mac laughed and patted the seat beside him. "Come here."

She shook her head. "Thanks. I'll just stay here."

"I said come here!" He grabbed her arm and yanked

her across the seat with such force that the sleeve of her blouse tore.

Tears sprang to her eyes and she cried out. "You don't have to be so rough!"

"Maybe next time you'll listen." He stared out the front window, his right hand still wrapped around her upper arm, his left hand clutching the knife.

She felt sick with terror, ice-cold and dizzy. But she refused to be cowed. She couldn't let him think he'd gotten the better of her. "Why are you doing this?" she asked. "I mean, what's the point?"

He looked at her, his eyes cold. Reptilian. "The point is, everyone has always underestimated me. Teachers in school, Dan and Drew, my ex-wife. Now they'll be sorry they didn't give me more credit."

The ironically cheerful electronic notes of "Lawyers, Guns and Money" made her jump. Mac's cell phone. He pulled it out of his pocket and glanced at the screen. "Private number. Want to bet it's the cops?"

"How did they get your number?"

He laughed. "They're the cops." He punched the keypad and put the phone to his ear. "Hello… Yes, this is him… I wouldn't do that if I were you. I've got a hostage. A young woman… That's right. I want a plane ticket to Chile and two hundred and fifty thousand dollars in unmarked bills. Tell my partners to consider that my buyout. Cheap at twice the price. I'll give you until nine o'clock. And don't try to sneak up on me, either." His gaze met Lexie's. "If you try anything, I'll cut the girl's throat."

He clicked off the phone and stuffed it back into his pocket. It immediately began ringing again, the cheerful tune sounding macabre under the circumstances. He switched it off.

She turned away from him and choked back a sob. "What do I have to do with any of this?" she asked.

"You're a lousy liar, did you know that?"

The sirens shut off, though her ears still rang with their echo. She watched him out of the corner of her eye. "What do you mean?"

"The eyes give it away every time." He tapped the side of his head, next to his eyes. "I learned that a long time ago. When someone's lying, they look up and away from the person they're talking to. You do it. Everybody does it. Except me. I trained myself not to do it." He smiled. "I trained myself like a warrior going into battle." He turned the knife so sunlight flashed off the blade.

Okay, he was seriously creeping her out. But she had to stay calm. She had to keep him talking. "Why did you go to so much trouble?"

His gaze shifted to her for a second, then darted away. "You figured it out. I'll give you that. You recognized that I was smart enough to pull this off. Not like Danny. 'Mac's just a dumb jock.' I bet that's what he told you."

She remained silent, afraid to look away from the knife. Somewhere in the distance she heard voices. The police?

"But you weren't sure, were you? Not until you read the magazine article. You knew then, didn't you?"

"Knew what?"

"Don't play dumb with me!" His rage resurfaced. He waved the knife in front of her face. She shrank back, strangling a cry. "You figured out I was the one selling the formulas to Jackson Labs."

"In exchange for knives."

"Valuable knives." He admired the Bowie. "We're not talking everyday cutlery. We're talking about important, historic weaponry."

She tried to take a deep breath, but her lungs refused to expand much. "So you traded the formulas for the knives to add to your collection. But why? Why ruin your own company?"

"It's not my company anymore." He shook his head.

"You're one of the partners."

"My name's on the letterhead. Danny and Drew let me think I have a say in how things run, but really they only keep me around to smile and shake hands and play the dumb good old boy for the shareholders."

"But you're a shareholder, aren't you?" she persisted.

He shrugged. "Only five percent."

"You're a partner and you only own five percent of the stock?"

"It used to be twenty-five percent, but the bitch's lawyers took most of that. They said she was entitled, since she was 'the face of Imari.'" His knuckles on the knife whitened. "If the company tanks, she'll be the one suffering now. All the more reason for me to help it along."

"Did the two of you meet when she was hired for the ad campaign?"

He nodded. "The ad agency asked me to show her around. I was feeling cocky and asked her to dinner and she said yes." He cut his eyes over to her. "I still looked like a college jock back then. She didn't have to be ashamed to be seen with me."

What were the police doing now? Were they going to give into his demands? Did that ever happen in real life? Or were they devising a plan of their own to capture

Mac—to save her? She had to do what she could to help. She had to keep him talking. "And you fell in love," she prompted.

He made a face. "Or something like it. Fell in lust, more like it. It didn't last." He picked at the edge of a parking sticker on the windshield with the tip of the knife blade.

"What happened?" What transformed a relationship from love to hate?

"I found out what she was really like. She turned out to be a money-grubbing harpy whose favorite word was 'more.' She wanted more money, more fame, more prestige. When I couldn't give her 'more' she dumped me."

"It's so sad." Had the same kind of thing happened with Nick and his ex? Did they start out in love, then end up despising each other? Is that why he never talked about her?

"You don't see me crying, do you? I was happy to be rid of her. And I'll be just as happy to be out from under Danny and Drew's condescension."

"But they're your best friends."

"To use a cliché—with friends like them, I don't need enemies." He looked out the side window, toward the elevator. "I should have told them to shut off the elevator. I don't want anybody coming up that way." He took the phone from his pocket again and switched it on, then hit the redial button.

A sharp voice answered. "Yeah, this is Mac Emerson. Tell somebody to shut down the elevator. I don't want anyone coming up that way…. No, I don't want to see you. I don't want to see anybody. When you've got the money and the ticket I asked for, then maybe we'll talk."

He listened a moment longer, then handed the phone to her. "He wants to talk to you."

She took the phone in shaking hands. "Y-yes?"

"Ms. Foster? Are you Lexie Foster?"

"Yes, that's me."

"Are you all right, Ms. Foster?"

She glanced at Mac. He was staring out the window, not watching her. "I'm scared," she whispered.

"We're doing our best to get you out safely. Try to stay calm. Does Emerson have a weapon?"

"He has a knife. A really big one."

"That's enough!" He wrenched the phone from her hand. "Yeah, I've got a knife," he barked into the phone. "And a .357 Magnum and an AK-47. I've also got enough dynamite to blow this whole block to the moon." He switched off the phone again and tossed it onto the dash.

Lexie frowned at him. "Is that true?" she asked. "About the dynamite and the guns?"

He settled into a more comfortable position, his expression smug. "That's the thing, isn't it? People can't tell when I'm lying." He glanced at her. "It's because I know what I'm doing. People always underestimate me."

She sank down in the seat, wishing she could make herself small enough to escape through the vents or the gap in the rolled-down window.

"What's with the scarf?"

Mac's question after a long silence startled her. She put a hand to the length of silk around her neck, avoiding the stiffened area where blood had dried. "I like to wear them."

"There you go lying again. Didn't I tell you I can always tell?" He studied her. "You could be making some kind of fashion statement, but you're young for that. On an older woman I'd say you were hiding wrinkles. Since you're not old, I think you're hiding something else."

"So? I have a scar."

"We have a new product coming out for that. It's supposed to be a miracle salve, to hide and even heal scars."

"I heard something about that."

"'Course, if you think about it, we're in the business of covering stuff up—signs of aging, wrinkles, blemishes, all the little flaws that make us human instead of plastic. Women cover them all up so they can look plastic—better than real."

He glanced at her. "You think my ex looks that good when she gets out of bed in the morning? She doesn't. It takes hours to get her looking like the face in the ads."

"What's her name?"

"What difference does it make. You can call her what I do—the Queen Bitch."

"No one ever says her name. I was curious."

"Her real name is Ginny with a G, but she changed it to Giselle. But hardly anybody uses that. To them, she's just a nameless face. Beautiful and empty, like her soul."

She hoped Mac had loved his wife as much as he hated her now. At least he would have some good times to look back on. Even Nick had admitted that much when she'd asked about his marriage.

Nick was nothing like Mac, of course. He didn't hate his ex. Whenever he spoke of her, he just looked…hurt. Because things hadn't worked out, or because he still loved her?

Where, exactly, did that leave his feelings for her? She'd tried not to think about that before, but now she had all kinds of time to ponder those questions she usually avoided.

She stared out the windshield, at the pink and orange glow of the sun setting behind the distant mountains.

Under other circumstances, she would have enjoyed the view. With the right person, she might have even called it romantic.

But there was no romance in the possibility of dying. Before, on that icy road, she hadn't really had enough time to think about the life she'd lived. That had come later, when she'd had her second chance in the hospital.

Now, she had too much time to contemplate the choices she'd made. She'd told herself before that she'd short-changed herself by not taking chances. Now she wondered if she'd cheated herself again, by not taking the *right* chances with Nick.

If she died here in this parking garage, would Nick ever know how much she'd come to love him? And how sorry she was she'd never worked up the nerve to tell him?

Oh, Nick, where are you right now? she wondered.

NICK WAS ON HIS FEET as soon as the plane landed, ignoring the announcement that everyone should remain in their seats until the plane had come to a complete stop. When the door opened, he pushed his way down the aisle. "Sorry, this is an emergency," he said as he headed for the jetway.

He raced out of the terminal and across the parking lot, not bothering to wait for the shuttle. As soon as he was in the car he switched on the radio, hoping for an update on the situation at Imari Industries.

Music, music, market report, weather, traffic, talk show… He hit the scan button repeatedly, but could learn nothing about Mac Emerson or Lexie.

He switched on his phone, and punched the number for his voice mailbox, hoping against hope Lexie had called to tell him she was free and waiting for him. When he heard her voice his heart leaped, but her words chilled him. "Call me. It's important."

What had she discovered that was so urgent? If he'd been around to take her call, could he have prevented Mac taking her hostage? He gripped the steering wheel with both hands, hunched forward, giant pincers of tension squeezing the back of his neck. "Hang on, Lexie. Just hang on," he muttered, over and over again under his breath, an incantation to ward off the fear that threatened to choke him.

Emergency flashers on, he sped toward downtown, an explanation ready if anyone tried to stop him. But no one did. Three blocks from the Imari building he came up against a police roadblock. Abandoning his car on a side street, he ran back to the cop on duty.

"Sir, you can't—"

"My girlfriend is the woman Mac Emerson is holding hostage," he said. He flashed his old badge for the Houston Police Department, careful to keep his thumb over the hole punched through the corner. "I know Mac. I think I can talk to him."

"Sure, Officer Delaney. Let me just call—"

He pushed past the cop, headed for the cluster of uniformed and plainclothes officers gathered near the entrance to the parking garage. As he neared them, he recognized Dan Ventura and Andrew Jeppson in their midst.

Ventura pushed forward to meet him. "I've been trying to contact you all afternoon," he said. "I don't know how this happened."

"I've been on a flight from Houston." He glanced up at the looming concrete layer cake of the garage. "What's going on?"

"Mac and Lexie are in his truck on the top level. He's

asking for two hundred and fifty thousand dollars and a ticket to Chile. He says he has knives, guns and dynamite."

Nick ignored the extra shot of fear at Ventura's words. "He collects guns as well as knives?"

Ventura shook his head. "As far as I knew, he was only interested in knives. But then, I never expected him to do something like this, either."

"Are you the boyfriend?" A dark-suited man about Nick's age approached.

"Nick Delaney. I'm Lexie's boyfriend. And her boss." He offered his hand.

"Lieutenant Jim Brewer. If you're her boss, then you're the detective Mr. Ventura was telling us about."

"That's right. I was with Houston PD before that." He looked up toward the top level of the garage. "What's going on up there?"

"Nothing much right now. We've got a spotter in the building across the street. Emerson and your girlfriend are just sitting in the truck."

"Any weapons?"

"He's got a knife. No sign of a gun, but he could be keeping it out of sight."

"Is Lexie all right?"

"She appears to be. We talked to her on the phone for a bit and she seemed okay. Scared, but okay."

He didn't want to think about Lexie scared. Her voice message still hammered at him. *Call me. It's important.* Guilt over not being there to help her when she needed him weighed him down. "How did this happen?" he asked the lieutenant. "Why is he holding her?"

"We're not sure about that yet. I understand she was helping you with an investigation involving Imari?"

"Yes, I was hired by Daniel Ventura to investigate the possibility that someone in the company was sharing top secret product formulas with Imari's chief competitor, Jackson Labs."

Brewer's attention shifted to Ventura. "Did you suspect Mr. Emerson of being involved in this?"

Ventura shook his head. "I wouldn't have thought he was capable of that kind of thing." Ventura's olive skin was washed the color of a boiled egg and his whole face seemed to sag. "Mac was always so…placid."

"But he collected knives." A man whose office practically bristled with steel blades was not someone Nick would ever have pegged as "placid." He turned to Ventura. "Did anything happen at the office today? Anything that would have set Mac off like this?"

Ventura shook his head. "No. I still don't believe Mac would have done this to us."

"I believe it." Jeppson moved to stand with them. "Sometimes I would catch him watching me and his eyes were so…so empty."

Nick had seen eyes like that before, eyes of men without a conscience or concern for anyone but themselves. Eyes of men who would kill anyone who got in their way. He clenched his hands into fists. "Someone needs to get up there and get her away from him."

"We're doing everything to see that Ms. Foster is safe." The lieutenant put a hand on his shoulder. "The best thing you can do is go to a safe place and wait." He signaled to a uniformed officer. "Officer Terry, will you escort Detective Delaney to his car?"

Nick knew what Brewer was doing. Hadn't he used the same lines himself? Get the family and friends away from the scene, where they couldn't interfere and cause trouble. The police knew best how to handle these things.

Except as far as he could see, they weren't handling them. He straightened his coat and manufactured a grateful tone of voice and a docile look. "Thanks, Lieutenant. Mr. Ventura knows how to reach me if you need me for anything else."

He went quietly with the officer, pretending to cooperate. But with every step, he was formulating his own plan. He hadn't been there to help Lexie avoid this situation, but he was going to do everything he could to get her out of it.

"THOSE COPS better hurry up. I'm hungry." Mac shifted in his seat and rubbed his stomach.

"We could order a pizza," Lexie said, only half joking.

"No way. They'd send up a cop instead of the delivery boy. Better to go hungry." He checked his watch. "It won't be long now."

How long? She didn't want to know. She closed her eyes and leaned her head back against the seat. They hadn't heard anything from the police in hours. As far as she could tell, no one was even attempting to contact them. What would happen when the deadline arrived? Would Mac stab her or slit her throat and try to make his getaway? Would they both die in a hail of gunfire?

The thing that surprised her most about all of this was how afraid she still was to die. She'd have thought after her previous near-death experience that some of that fear of the unknown would have faded.

But it wasn't the unknown that frightened her, she decided. It was leaving before she'd had a chance to live the life she wanted to live. There were so many things on her list she hadn't done yet. So many places to see, things to learn.

People to love. She swallowed tears, thinking of Nick. After almost dying in that car accident, she'd been so worried about things she hadn't done that she hadn't given any thought to things she hadn't said.

Things like *I love you* and *I'm sorry if I hurt you* and *Please give me another chance.*

Give *us* another chance.

That was what living was all about, wasn't it? Every day was another chance to get it right. She wanted to keep on having those other chances. She didn't want a middle-aged loser who'd screwed up his life to end hers before she was ready.

She opened her eyes and turned to Mac. "If they give you the money and the plane ticket, are you really going to let me go?"

He turned his head to look at her, all the life gone out of his eyes, all expression wiped from his face. "What do you think?"

"I don't know." She swallowed past the knot of fear that choked her. "I think you should."

He turned away again. "I don't know about that. I think the chances of either one of us getting out of this alive are pretty slim, don't you?"

What had happened to the cockiness and disdain he'd displayed earlier? This resigned attitude frightened her even more. "I thought you wanted to go to Chile," she said. "To take the money and get away."

"You haven't been listening. Can't you manage something as simple as that?" He glared at her, his face flushed. "What I want is for people to give me credit for having a brain. To admit that I'm capable of pulling off a grand scheme. And because they didn't give me credit, I want them to suffer."

She didn't expect a crazy person to think logically, but this was so twisted. "So if you die, how will that make them suffer?"

"The scandal will make the company tank. And they'll spend the rest of their lives wondering what they could have done to prevent the disaster."

The sheer stupidity of his scheme angered her. "Fine," she snapped. "You die. I want to live."

He leaned forward over the steering wheel and began picking at the parking sticker with the knife once more. "I guess we'll find out soon enough if you get your wish."

NICK GOT IN HIS CAR and drove away from the Imari building. He could see Officer Terry watching him, to make sure he left. She'd report back to her lieutenant that Nick wasn't going to be a problem for them.

He drove to his office, and went straight to his desk, where he unlocked the drawer that contained his service revolver and ammunition. He checked the gun, loaded it and slipped on the shoulder holster. The hard weight of it against his ribs brought back memories of all those nights on the hot streets of Houston. Too bad he didn't still have his Kevlar vest, too.

But then, Lexie didn't have a vest, did she? She didn't have any kind of protection from a nut with a knife and maybe a gun. He drove back toward downtown, giving a wide berth to the Imari building, though at every intersection he looked between buildings and saw the clusters of police cars and news vans that marked the crime scene.

He parked in an alley six blocks away and started toward the site on foot. He searched his memory of the layout of the offices and identified a service entrance leading onto the loading dock. It was the entrance farthest from the parking garage, but a walkway on the fourth floor led to the garage. Both these portals were likely guarded, but he hoped to evade the guards.

The loading dock had a single uniformed officer stationed by the door. He looked bored, slumped against the brick wall. Nick straightened his shoulder and approached. He nodded to the officer and flashed his badge, moving back his coat just enough to give a glimpse of the regulation firearm. "Brewer sent me for Emerson's computer." Computers were as good as picking a suspect's brain these days, and often the first piece of evidence the cops went for.

"Yes sir, Detective Delaney." The cop didn't question. Nick acted as if he knew what he was doing. He looked official and dropped the right name. The cop even held the door open for him.

He took the stairs two at a time and headed straight for the walkway to the garage. No guard there. With the building sealed off, they probably hadn't seen a need.

Keeping low so a police spotter wouldn't see him and report his presence to the crowd of law enforcement below, he scooted through the walkway to the garage. He paused to let his eyes adjust to the dimness, and thought about where Lexie was in relationship to where he was standing now.

He started across the concrete to the next set of steps, but froze only a few feet in. His footsteps echoed around him, even when he tiptoed. Not hesitating, he stripped off his shoes and proceeded in his stocking feet. The floor was cold, the chill seeping through his socks, but he scarcely noticed.

At the bottom of the steps to the top floor, he stopped and took out the gun.

Keeping in the shadows along the edge of the ramp, he moved in a crouch until he was eye-level with the floor of the rooftop parking area. He spotted Lexie's car right away, sitting among half a dozen other cars not far from the walkway, the driver's side door open, the dome light on. Turning his head, he found Emerson's truck, by itself in the back corner. From this angle, he couldn't see the people in it. He hoped they couldn't see him.

He crouched lower, assessing the situation. He needed to move onto their level, to take cover behind the other parked cars. Emerson was no doubt watching the ramp. How could he distract him without raising his suspicions?

He looked across the garage, to the corner on this level that corresponded to the space above where Emerson's truck was parked. An elevator bank sat silent.

Stealthily, Nick made his way to the elevator. He punched the up button and waited.

The rumble of the elevator car moving up the shaft was as loud as approaching artillery. No way Emerson could have missed it. As soon as the doors started to open, Nick hit the up button and turned to race to the ramp.

Pistol ready, he darted across the football-field wide expanse of open concrete and dove between two parked cars. When he came up and looked over at the truck, Emerson was standing beside it, staring at the elevator, which stood open and empty. "Is this some kind of trick?" he bellowed, turning back to the truck.

"Maybe it started on its own," Lexie said.

Nick stared at her, heart pounding. She looked okay. Tired. A little stressed, but okay. She wasn't bleeding, at least not from the chest up, and she sounded strong. *Hang on*, he thought. *Just hang on.*

He was on the passenger side of her car. Through the window he could see the contents of her purse spilled out across the seat, and a magazine, open to an article titled "Cosmetics magnate specializes in Civil War weaponry." He squinted, trying to bring the small print into focus.

Marcus Jackson, founder of cosmetics giant Jackson Labs, has one of the premier Civil War weapons collections in the world, including two rare Rezin Bowie-made knives with scabbards.

A picture of Mac Emerson standing before his wall of weapons flashed through Nick's mind. *I'm starting to specialize in Civil War pieces,* he'd said. *I have my eye on a particularly fine example of a Bowie knife I hope to acquire soon.*

Nick had a feeling Jackson's collection had been reduced by at least one now. Had he traded the valuable knife for Imari's product formulas?

The truck door slammed as Mac got in. Nick gripped the pistol and contemplated his shot. At this distance, through the windshield of the truck, he couldn't risk it. With a rifle, maybe, but with Lexie sitting so close to Mac he couldn't take the chance.

Why hadn't he shot while Mac was standing outside the truck? How long could he crouch here and wait for someone—either Mac or the police—to make a move?

LEXIE HAD TO BITE her lip to keep from crying out when she saw Nick run across the garage toward the parked cars. Even now, it was all she could do not to look over at him. Mac had obviously been too focused on the elevator to have seen Nick before. But he was jumpy now, convinced the cops were trying to trick him. She didn't want to make him any more suspicious.

She knew Nick was over there, but she had no idea what he planned to do. She tried to think how she could help him get her out of here.

"I have to go to the bathroom," she announced loudly. It wasn't a lie. Her bladder had been nagging at her for over an hour, but until now it had seemed like the least of her concerns.

"You'll have to wait," Mac said.

"I can't wait." She squirmed. "I really have to go."

"Too bad."

She scowled at him. The jerk was probably enjoying her suffering. "If you don't let me out to go I'll do it right here in your truck."

He smirked. "You wouldn't do that."

"As long as I've been holding it, I don't really have a choice." The last thing she wanted was to pee her pants, but if it meant getting out of here alive, she'd go for it.

Mac's smirk faded. "There's no bathroom up here."

"I'm desperate. I'll go behind those parked cars over there." She nodded toward Nick's hiding place.

"Not by yourself, you won't."

"So go with me. I told you, I'm desperate."

He grabbed her arm and nudged open the door with the hand that held the knife. "Okay. But don't try anything."

She'd been sitting in the truck so long her legs almost gave out when she first tried to stand. She steadied herself against the truck. Mac pulled her upright. "Hurry it up."

She hurried all right, almost dragging him toward the cluster of cars. She watched for Nick out of the corner of her eye, but he'd vanished. She took a deep breath, telling herself she had to trust him now.

"This is good enough." They'd barely reached the first cars when the tip of the knife dug into her side. "Go here."

Before she had time to contemplate how embarrassing this was, she hiked up her skirt and acted as if she were going to pull down her panties. She glared at Mac over her shoulder. "Turn your head."

"Maybe I don't want to," he said, his face sullen.

"I can't go with you watching me!"

He shook his head, but looked away, keeping the knife firmly against her side.

She sighed and squatted on the garage floor. What to do now? Actually peeing hadn't been part of her plan.

Apparently Mac had no such dilemma. To her astonishment, she heard the sound of a zipper lowering, followed by a steady stream against the front tire of the nearest car.

She jumped up, ignoring the knife that cut into her side, and took off on a run across the garage, resisting the urge to look back.

Mac roared and whirled toward her, hindered by his unzipped pants sagging around his hips. At that moment Nick stepped out and stuck his gun in Mac's side. "Don't move," he said. "I won't hesitate to blow you away."

Lexie stopped on the far side of the garage and turned to watch the two men. Mac covered his face with his hands and began to sob. "Go tell Lieutenant Brewer I've got him," Nick said, his gaze fixed on Emerson.

Giving them a wide berth, she made her way back to the truck, and found Mac's cell phone on the dash. Struggling to hold it steady, she hit the redial button. "This is Lexie Foster," she said when a man answered. "It's over."

18

THE POLICE SURROUNDED Emerson and took him away in handcuffs. Nick found Lexie still standing beside the truck and pulled her into his arms. They clung together for a long moment, not saying anything. He didn't know if he could even find words for what he was feeling right then—enormous relief that she was safe, coupled with the sickening realization of what could have gone wrong. At last he managed to pry his arms from around her enough to look at her. "Are you okay?"

She nodded. "I'm fine."

His gaze fixed on the thin brown line against her throat, and the smear of dried blood on her blouse, and rage rose in his throat. He smoothed his hands down her arms, fighting for control. "You're hurt." His voice shook. He cleared his throat and tried again. "You should see a doctor."

She gave him a wobbly smile and put one hand to her throat. "It's okay, really. Just a little scratch. But I really do have to go to the bathroom."

He looked up and saw Lieutenant Brewer headed toward them. "I think now would be the perfect time to leave," he said, steering her toward the elevator.

Brewer waylaid them just as Nick was punching the

down button. "I ought to arrest you for interfering with police work," he said.

Nick nodded. "I know how it is. You're official. You have to play it safe—do what's best for the public and your officers as well as for the hostage. Me, I'm just a civilian. I was worried about my girlfriend, unwilling to wait. I took matters into my own hands without your knowledge." Later, at the press conference, Brewer could use Nick's words as his own.

"You could have gotten yourself and your girlfriend killed."

He nodded, locking his knees to keep them from shaking. "But I didn't."

Brewer turned to Lexie. "Are you all right?"

She nodded. "I'll be fine."

"We didn't find a gun on him or in his truck."

"He didn't have one. Just the knife."

"The knife he got from Jackson?" Nick asked.

"Yes. He traded the secret formulas for knives to add to his collection."

"We'll need to get a statement from you right away," Brewer said.

"Fine. I just want to, uh, freshen up a bit first."

"All right. We'll talk to you shortly." He eyed Nick. "We'll need a statement from you also. After that, I don't want to see you again."

"Yeah." He could happily live the rest of his life without a repeat of the past few hours.

He escorted Lexie downstairs and waited outside the ladies' room. When she emerged, she looked remarkably refreshed. She'd washed her face and her throat, smoothed her hair and clothes, and except for a lingering weariness around her eyes, and the blood stain on her scarf, you'd never know she'd been through an ordeal.

She gave him a shy smile. "I haven't really thanked you for saving me, have I? You took a big risk for me."

"You're worth a big risk." He put his arms around her and gathered her close. "What happened to not doing anything risky while I was away?"

"I didn't do anything. But I guess Mac saw me with the magazine and put two and two together. Apparently he'd already found out that I was working for you and that you were a detective."

"I saw the magazine in your car. Is that the one you're talking about?"

She nodded. "When I saw the article about Marcus Jackson, I knew Mac had to be the one trading the secrets. The article said Jackson collected Civil War weapons, and Mac had just acquired several new Civil War-era knives. It all fit together."

"To think he'd ruin the company he helped found for the sake of a bunch of antique knives."

"It wasn't just that. He wanted revenge. He wanted to do something that would hurt his two friends and his ex-wife, who were the majority stockholders."

"He told you that?"

She nodded. "Apparently he felt Ventura and Jeppson had always underestimated him. They thought he was a dumb jock. His ex had apparently taken him to the cleaners in the divorce. She ended up with most of the company stock."

"He obviously wasn't very smart if he thought taking you hostage was really going to accomplish anything."

"I think maybe he wanted to get caught. On one hand,

he wanted to gloat about what he'd gotten away with, but on the other I think he wanted to be stopped. He wasn't a happy man."

"I'm happy he's out of our lives now. When I heard on the flight home that you'd been taken hostage, I didn't know if I'd make it back to Denver without going crazy from worrying."

She pulled away, her cheerfulness a little forced. "How did your trip to Houston go?"

"It went okay." He glanced at her. "I went to see my ex-wife."

"Oh?" She looked away, her face pale. "I guess I had the impression that you two weren't speaking."

"We weren't. But that was all my doing. I thought it was about time I corrected that." That was the first of many mistakes he intended to make up for. And he'd continue now with Lexie. "I wanted to talk to you about that, too."

"That's great." She avoided his gaze. "But I'd better go talk to that lieutenant now. I'm sure he's waiting for my statement."

"Wait. Let me come with you."

"That's okay. I know how it is when you've been out of town. You probably have a ton of stuff to do."

With a too-bright smile, she was gone, leaving him standing alone outside the restrooms. He'd been all ready to tell her how much he loved her, to beg her to stay with him, and all she could do was run away.

When he'd been holding her, he was sure he had a chance with her. But maybe another close call with death had reminded her of how much she still wanted to do.

Apparently loving him wasn't on her list.

LEXIE STOOD on the sidewalk outside Delaney Investigations, mustering the nerve to go inside and talk to Nick. She'd given this a lot of thought, and she wanted to do it right. Yesterday, when her emotions were in such turmoil from everything that had happened, she had been afraid she'd say the wrong thing.

But now she'd had time to prepare. To make plans.

She pushed open the door and headed straight for Nick's office. He looked up, apparently surprised to see her. "Hey. I didn't expect you in today. You sure you feel up to working?"

"Of course. I feel great. Nothing like a brush with death to make you appreciate getting up in the morning. Could we talk a minute?"

"Sure." He stood and cleared off a chair for her, then sat down behind the desk. His hair and clothes were both rumpled and the lines around his eyes were more pronounced, as if he'd had a rough night.

She sat with her purse in her lap, clutching it like a life preserver. Anything to hide the shaking in her hands. "I wanted to thank you again for what you did yesterday," she said. "It was really brave of you."

"I'm just glad it worked out all right."

"I'm sorry I didn't stay around to talk to you afterward, but I was still shaken up. I wanted to be alone and think."

"Sure. I understand." But his eyes refused to meet hers, focusing instead on the far wall.

Okay, maybe she deserved that, for running out on him yesterday. She only hoped what she had to say now would make him a little more forgiving. "I wanted to give you this." She took an envelope from her purse and pushed it across the desk toward him.

He stared at it, turning it over and over in his hand. "Is this your resignation?"

"Why don't you open it and see?"

He ran his thumb under the flap and pulled out a sheaf of papers. Frowning, he looked at her. "These are your tickets to Spain."

"They're tickets to Spain, but look again."

He opened the ticket folder and thumbed through it, stopping halfway through. "Why is my name on this ticket?"

She fidgeted in the chair. "I want you to go with me."

"What?" He laid aside the envelope. "I already told you—I can't drop everything and follow you to Spain."

Not exactly the enthusiastic reception she'd hoped for. She smiled, though it felt more like a grimace, determined to keep trying, though he certainly wasn't making this easy. "Not drop everything. It's only for a week. And not follow. Come with." She leaned toward him. "As in, by my side."

His fingers drummed the desk, his expression still guarded. "I thought you were going to stay as long as you could, go where the wind led you."

"That was before yesterday. I think now I'm ready to stop rushing to cram as many things and accomplishments into my life as I can. I want to slow down a little and enjoy what's in front of me more, instead of always looking ahead."

His fingers stilled. "And where do I come in to this?"

She took a deep breath. One of the things on her list was sky-diving, but taking this plunge had to be at least as scary. And the outcome was much less certain. "I love you, Nick."

He nodded. "I know you do. I love you, too."

The anchor that had been fastened around her ankles released, and she felt as if she might float up out of the chair. "That's wonderful. Fantastic!"

He leaned toward her, his expression still grave. "But is that enough? I don't want to make another mistake like the one I made with Monica. And I don't want you to be unhappy if you feel tied down."

She shook her head. "I thought all I wanted from you was a brief affair, but I was wrong. The more time I spent with you, the better I got to know you, the more I knew I'd found someone special." She reached out and grabbed his hand. "I don't want to let you go. Ever. Trapped in that truck with Mac, all I could think of was how close I'd come to screwing up and leaving you behind. I got another second chance and I don't intend to blow this one."

He turned his palm up and wrapped his hand around hers. The pained look left his eyes, replaced by a new softness. "I'm the one who almost screwed up," he said, his voice rough. He cleared his throat. "Do you know the reason I went to Houston to see Monica?"

She shook her head. "I wondered."

"I wanted to find out what went wrong between us. What I'd done. I wanted to know if I was repeating the same mistakes with you."

"Why would you think that?"

"Because you were leaving me, too." He released her hand and sat back. "For all the things we'd shared and the connection we had, you were willing to walk away and I was desperate to find a way to stop you."

"And you found out how from your ex?"

"She told me I'd never told her how I was really feeling. That I'd shut her out and kept too much to myself." He shook his head. "It sounded so simple. And so hard, too."

"I know."

She got up and went to him. He pushed back his chair

and she sat in his lap and wrapped his arms around her. "All I could think of all the way home from Houston was that I'd never told you I loved you. I've spent the past twenty-four hours rehearsing things to say to try to make you stay here with me."

"You don't have to make me stay. I want to."

"I love you," he said again, and laughed. "Now that I've said it, I don't think I can say it enough."

"I'll never get tired of hearing it." She kissed his cheek. "I love you."

He smiled at her. "What do you think of Spain for a honeymoon destination?"

Her breath caught in her throat. "I—I think it sounds very romantic." She rested her palm against his chest, over his heart. "Do you think you could work with your wife?"

"I think we make a great team. But what about the rest of the items on your list?"

She snuggled closer. She'd have to change a few things on that list now. No more six affairs. One had been enough to teach her all she needed to know about herself, and about love. "I'm thinking maybe we should make a new list…of things to do together."

* * * * *

Look for Cindi Myers's
THE BIRDMAN'S DAUGHTER
coming in April 2006 from Harlequin Next.
And watch for Cindi's return to
Harlequin Blaze in September 2006.

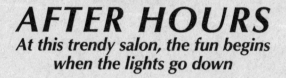

If you enjoyed what you just read,
then we've got an offer you can't resist!

Take 2 bestselling
love stories FREE!

Plus get a FREE surprise gift!

Clip this page and mail it to Harlequin Reader Service®

IN U.S.A.	**IN CANADA**
3010 Walden Ave.	P.O. Box 609
P.O. Box 1867	Fort Erie, Ontario
Buffalo, N.Y. 14240-1867	L2A 5X3

YES! Please send me 2 free Harlequin® Blaze™ novels and my free surprise gift. After receiving them, if I don't wish to receive anymore, I can return the shipping statement marked cancel. If I don't cancel, I will receive 6 brand-new novels each month, before they're available in stores! In the U.S.A., bill me at the bargain price of $3.99 plus 25¢ shipping and handling per book and applicable sales tax, if any*. In Canada, bill me at the bargain price of $4.47 plus 25¢ shipping and handling per book and applicable taxes**. That's the complete price and a savings of at least 10% off the cover prices—what a great deal! I understand that accepting the 2 free books and gift places me under no obligation ever to buy any books. I can always return a shipment and cancel at any time. Even if I never buy another book from Harlequin, the 2 free books and gift are mine to keep forever.

151 HDN D7ZZ
351 HDN D72D

Name	(PLEASE PRINT)	
Address	Apt.#	
City	State/Prov.	Zip/Postal Code

Not valid to current Harlequin® Blaze™ subscribers.

Want to try two free books from another series?
Call 1-800-873-8635 or visit www.morefreebooks.com.

* Terms and prices subject to change without notice. Sales tax applicable in N.Y.
** Canadian residents will be charged applicable provincial taxes and GST.
  All orders subject to approval. Offer limited to one per household.
  ® and ™ are registered trademarks owned and used by the trademark owner and/or its licensee.

BLZ05   ©2005 Harlequin Enterprises Limited.

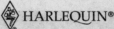

COMING NEXT MONTH

#243 OBSESSION Tori Carrington
Dangerous Liaisons, Bk. 2
Anything can happen in the Quarter.... Hotel owner Josie Villefranche knows that
better than most. Ever since a woman was murdered in her establishment, business
has drastically declined. She's very tempted to allow sexy Drew Morrison to help her
take her mind off her troubles—until she learns he wants much more than just a night
in her bed....

#244 WHAT HAVE I DONE FOR ME LATELY? Isabel Sharpe
It's All About Attitude
Jenny Hartmann's sizzling bestseller *What Have I Done for Me Lately?* is causing an
uproar across the country. And now Jenny's about to take her own advice—by having
a sexual fling with Ryan Masterson. What Jenny isn't prepared for is that the former
bad boy is good in bed—and even better at reading between the lines!

#245 SHARE THE DARKNESS Jill Monroe
FBI agent Ward Cassidy thinks Hannah Garret is a criminal. And Hannah suspects Ward
is working for her ex-fiancé, the man who now wants her dead. But when Hannah and Ward
get caught for hours in a hot, darkened elevator, the sensual pull of their bodies tells them
all they *really* need to know....

#246 MIDNIGHT OIL Karen Kendall
After Hours, Bk. 1
It's the trendiest salon in Miami...and landlord Troy Barrington is determined to shut
it down. As part owner and massage therapist, Peggy Underwood can't let him—and
his ego—win. So she'll use all of the sensual, er, *spa* tools at her disposal to change
his mind.

#247 AFTERNOON DELIGHT Mia Zachary
Rei Davis is a tough-minded judge who wishes someone could see her softer side.
Chris London is a lighthearted matchmaker who wishes someone would take him
seriously. When Rei walks into Lunch Meetings, the dating service Chris owns, and
the computer determines that they're a perfect match, sparks fly! But will all their
wishes come true?

#248 INTO TEMPTATION Jeanie London
The White Star, Bk. 4
It's the sexiest game of cat and mouse she's ever played. MI6 agent Lindy Gardner is
determined to capture Joshua Benedict—and the stolen amulet in his possession. The
man is leading her on a sensual chase across two continents that will only make his
surrender oh, so satisfying.